A Ghost Magnet

"Listen, I've got to talk to you about what happened today."

"What *did* happen today? What the heck were you thinking of, saying you're going to interview the Snapping Turtle?"

"That's just it, Dub," Allie answered in a small voice. "I wasn't thinking. I didn't say it. I mean, I didn't mean to say it. It just came out."

Now it was Dub's turn to stop walking. "You mean—" His eyes grew big. "Like before?"

Allie nodded.

"Another ghost?" Dub asked in a hushed voice.

Allie shrugged. "I don't know. But it seemed . . . the same."

"It's so weird, Al. It's like you attract ghosts. Like you're some kind of—*ghost magnet*."

The Ghost
and Mrs. Hobbs

The Ghost and Mrs. Hobbs

Cynthia DeFelice

HarperTrophy®
An Imprint of HarperCollins*Publishers*

Harper Trophy® is a registered trademark of HarperCollins Publishers Inc.

The Ghost and Mrs. Hobbs
Copyright © 2001 by Cynthia C. DeFelice
This work was originally published in 2001 by Farrar, Straus and Giroux, LLC.
Published by arrangement with Farrar, Straus and Giroux.

Library of Congress Cataloging-in-Publication Data
DeFelice, Cynthia C.
    The ghost and Mrs. Hobbs / Cynthia DeFelice. — 1st Harper Trophy ed.
        p.   cm.
    Summary: Hindered by a fight with her friend Dub and a series of mysterious
fires, eleven-year-old Allie investigates the fire seventeen years earlier that
claimed the lives of the husband and infant son of a school cafeteria worker, as
well as the handsome young man whose ghost asks Allie for help.
    ISBN 0-06-001172-6 (pbk.)
    [1. Ghosts—Fiction.   2. Arson—Fiction.   3. Jealousy—Fiction.
4. Schools—Fiction.   5. Mystery and detective stories.]   I. Title.
PZ7.D3597 Ge   2003   2002027344
[Fic]—dc21   CIP
                                                                            AC

First Harper Trophy edition, 2003
❖
Visit us on the World Wide Web!
www.harperchildrens.com

For Zoe,
who wanted a touch of romance!

The Ghost
and Mrs. Hobbs

one

Allie Nichols knew she was dreaming, but that didn't make the feeling of being trapped in a burning building any less terrifying. Flames surrounded her, scorching her skin, licking at her clothing and hair, sucking the oxygen from the room and from her lungs until she couldn't breathe. Frantic, blinded by smoke and coughing, she crawled across an endless floor toward a door. When she got there, the doorknob was too hot to touch. Someone was on the other side of that door, someone who would die unless she got through. But she couldn't, she couldn't. No matter how hard she tried, she couldn't reach the door, and it was going to be too late. And then—oh no, no, no!—the ceiling came crashing down and she was trapped, and then it *was* too late.

Allie woke up with a sob, drenched in sweat, the taste of ashes in her mouth. She lay still, willing her heart to stop pounding, but the nightmarish urgency and the feelings of fear and desperation lingered. Not wanting to be alone, but not wanting to disturb her parents, either, she went down the hall to her little brother Michael's room and crawled into bed with him.

"Mmmm," he murmured sleepily.

"Okay if I get in with you for a while, Mikey?" Allie whispered.

"Mmmm."

Allie snuggled up to the curve of his warm, little four-year-old body and took a deep breath. What a dreadful dream! At first it had seemed to be happening to her. But then, in the strange logic of nightmares, she had felt as if she were watching and it was someone else who was struggling toward that door.

Who? And who was on the other side, waiting to be rescued? She couldn't imagine, and at last grew tired of trying. Concentrating instead on the soft, even rhythm of Michael's breathing, she finally fell back to sleep.

The vividness and power of the dream were still with her, though, when she woke up to find Michael staring at her curiously. "How come you're here?" he asked.

"Don't you remember when I came in?"

Michael shook his head. "Did you have a bad dream?" he asked.

Allie nodded.

"About the tree monster?" Michael asked, his eyes growing big and round.

"No," said Allie, giving him a hug. "Not that dumb old monster. Remember? I told him he better not show up in your dreams or mine ever again *or else*."

Michael giggled. "Oh yeah. Dumb monster!"

"My dream is all gone now," Allie said, lying. Michael had a powerful imagination, just as she did. Sometimes he scared himself with his own fantasies. She didn't want to get him started again on his old, bad dreams about the tree outside his window coming to grab him while he slept. "Come on. Let's get some breakfast."

The dream stayed in the back of Allie's mind while she and Michael ate their cereal.

When their parents joined them in the kitchen, Michael announced proudly, "Allie was in my bed this morning."

"Trouble sleeping, sweetie?" Allie's mother asked with concern.

"A little," Allie answered evasively. She had been trying especially hard not to give her parents any reason to worry about her, since she'd nearly died during a class field trip to Fossil Glen just three weeks before.

Allie had never figured out quite how to explain to

them that the whole Fossil Glen episode had come about because she'd been helping a *ghost*. Now that some time had gone by, it seemed even harder to bring up the subject. Allie was afraid that her parents would start worrying again that she didn't know the difference between fantasy and reality.

It was asking a lot to expect them to believe that the ghost of an eleven-year-old girl named Lucy Stiles, who had been murdered, had come to Allie for help in proving it. Allie didn't know if *she'd* be able to accept it if it hadn't happened to her.

The only person who knew the whole story was her best friend, Dub Whitwell. Thank goodness for Dub, she thought, not for the first time. If it wasn't for him, she might worry that she was crazy.

As Allie walked to school, her frightful dream replayed in her mind. She tried to concentrate during language arts, but the dream kept drifting through her thoughts, accompanied by the faint smell of smoke.

She was finally roused from her reverie when Mr. Henry announced that the school's annual Elders Day celebration was coming up the following week. A groan rose from the class.

Mr. Henry just smiled. "I know, I know," he said calmly. "You've done Elders Day in May of every school year since kindergarten. And you're tired of it. So I was thinking that instead of having each of you bring a special older friend to school for the day, as you've done before, we'd do something different this year."

Joey Fratto let out a cheer. Karen Laver muttered, "This better be good," but, as always, she made her comment too soft for Mr. Henry to hear.

Allie sat up and listened attentively. Mr. Henry was the best sixth-grade teacher in the school, the best teacher she had ever had. He had a way of making almost every subject fun and interesting. No matter what Karen said, Allie had a feeling Mr. Henry's plan for Elders Day was going to mean excitement.

two

"So, Dub, who are you going to interview?" Allie asked. She and her classmates were eating lunch in the cafeteria, following Mr. Henry's announcement that the kids would interview an older person and give an oral presentation.

Dub had just taken a huge bite of his sub sandwich. He struggled to chew and swallow so he could answer, but before he had a chance, Karen spoke up. "I don't know why we can't just skip stupid Elders Day now that we're in sixth grade," she said sulkily. "I mean, enough already."

"Well, at least Mr. Henry's letting us do something interesting this time," said Allie.

"Big deal," Karen replied. "It's just as boring."

Allie shrugged. Karen thought everything was boring.

"As far as I'm concerned," said Dub, "*anything* we do will be an improvement over last year."

Allie laughed, along with several other kids who had been in Dub's fifth-grade class to witness the previous year's fiasco. Like Allie, Dub had no grandparents living conveniently nearby, so he had been stuck with bringing his neighbor, old Louie Howell, to school for Elders Day. The trouble was that Louie was almost totally deaf.

Dub groaned. "That was a real nightmare."

"*A real white hair, you say?*" Imitating Louie Howell, Joey shouted in a high, whining voice, "*Who's got white hair? For the love of Myrtle, speak up, young man, and stop your mumbling!*"

Everyone at the lunch table cracked up. Dub said, "Compared to that, picking an elderly person to interview will be a piece of cake. And here's some free advice: Pick somebody who can hear your questions."

"So, Dub," Allie persisted, "who are you going to pick?"

"I'm going to ask Mr. Henry if it's okay to do the interview over the phone," Dub answered eagerly. "If he says yes, I want to call this cool old guy I met at the Cape last summer. He invents stuff using seaweed. So far he's made spaghetti sauce, wrinkle cream, and dog bones. Last summer he was making paste to hold his false teeth in."

"Gross!" squealed Pam Wright.

"He figures he's going to make millions on it," Dub added.

"Sure he is," said Karen scornfully.

"I think I'll bring my grandfather to school again," said Joey. "He was there the day that blimp, the whatchamacallit—the *Hindenburg*—blew up. It's a great story, the way he tells it."

"No fair," protested Karen. "You have to do the interview and make the presentation yourself."

"Nice try, though, Joey," said Allie with a smile.

"I think my aunt used to be a nurse in the coal mines or something," said Pam. "That could be kind of interesting."

Karen gave Pam a look, as if to say, You're not actually getting into this dumb idea, are you? She leaned back in her chair and tossed her braid over her shoulder. "I have no clue who to interview," she said. "I mean, my grandmother lives with us, but she's a total vegetable. All she ever does is watch the home shopping channel and order useless stuff that my mother has to send back."

Allie felt sorry for anyone who had to live with Karen. She figured Karen's grandmother kept the TV on so she wouldn't have to listen to Karen complaining all the time. But she kept her thoughts to herself.

Allie didn't care if Karen thought Mr. Henry's idea for Elders Day was boring. She had always been interested in people's stories, especially in the things they usually kept hidden. She was curious about what lay beneath the surface. She decided that she was going to find someone really fascinating to interview.

"Maybe I'll pick my Uncle Hal," said Brad Lewis. "Once he ate forty-seven pickled eggs and won a hundred bucks, and he won another contest for smashing beer cans on his forehead. I think he demolished thirty-three cans before he knocked himself out."

Everybody laughed, and Dub said, "Mr. Henry said this project might teach us about some milestones in history, and it looks like he was right."

"And get this," Brad added. "Every time he smashes a can, he hollers, 'Recycle *this*!' "

Allie was just opening her mouth to speak when a voice blurted, "Well, my subject is going to be Mrs. Hobbs."

Allie felt her eyes widen in astonishment. She looked around the lunch table to discover who had said such a foolish thing and saw that all of her classmates were turned toward *her*, their faces registering shock and disbelief.

Horrified voices whispered, "*Mrs. Hobbs*?"

"You've got to be kidding!"

"You're going to interview the Snapping Turtle?"

"Old Hobbling Hobbs?"

"That's not even funny, Al," said Dub, looking worried. "She *hates* kids."

Allie's hand flew to her mouth. Was she really the one who had spoken? What in the world was she thinking? Why had she said such a thing?

Mrs. Hobbs had worked in the cafeteria as long as Allie could remember. All the kids, even the sixth-graders, were terrified of her. Many of them, like Allie, brought their own lunches from home just so they wouldn't have to pass through the food line under her unblinking glare.

Allie glanced toward the front of the cafeteria and shuddered. There stood Mrs. Hobbs, her thin, wrinkled lips tightly clamped and her beady eyes darting from side to side, like a snapping turtle sizing up its next victim. As she ladled glops of food onto trays, her eyes seemed to devour each child who crept by.

The nickname Hobbling Hobbs referred to her peculiar, lurching gait, which had caused some kids to speculate that she wasn't human at all but a robot whose inner controls had gone haywire. Allie had seen kindergartners burst into tears at the mere sight of Mrs. Hobbs.

What was even more unsettling than the prospect of a one-on-one, face-to-face interview with Mrs. Hobbs was that Allie had blurted out this startling information without having any idea she was going to do it.

The last time something like that had happened was three weeks before, when Allie was being haunted by Lucy Stiles's ghost. The same chill she had felt then was creeping down her neck. A familiar feeling took hold of her, a mixture of excitement and dread.

Was it happening again?

three

On the way home from school that day, Karen and Pam caught up with Allie and Dub.

"I don't believe you, Allie," said Karen. "You have to announce you're going to interview the Snapping Turtle because you're so desperate to be the center of attention!"

"I am not!" said Allie indignantly. "I—" She stopped, flustered by the unfairness of Karen's attack. Besides, she couldn't explain why she'd blurted out such a bizarre thing, even if she'd wanted to do it.

"As if you're really going to talk to her," said Karen disdainfully.

"Don't let her get to you, Al," Dub said under his breath.

Allie knew Dub was right, but it wasn't easy to follow his advice. To make matters worse, Karen was accompanied by her faithful sidekick Pam, who went along with everything Karen said and did. Allie kept walking, waiting for Pam to chime in with her own nasty comment.

Sure enough, Pam did speak up next. "I think it's a pretty cool idea."

Allie was so surprised, she stopped walking to stare at Pam. It was amazing enough that Pam had contradicted Karen, but had she also said she thought the idea of interviewing Mrs. Hobbs was cool?

"It's awesome, actually," Pam went on, giving Allie what seemed to be a genuine smile. "*If* you survive, that is."

Allie let out a burst of laughter, both at Pam's unexpected friendliness and at the expression on Karen's face. She looked as if she'd just opened a beautiful package only to find it filled with used tissues.

"Way to go, Pam," Dub murmured. Louder, he said, "Of course we understand *you* wouldn't have the guts to do it, Karen."

"It isn't a question of guts, Dub Whitwell," said Karen furiously. "It's a question of brains. I'm not stupid enough—or desperate enough for attention— to even think about it." She turned to Allie and smiled wickedly. "But now that you've made your big announcement, I can't decide which will be more fun: seeing you try to worm your way out of it or watching you go through with it. Either way, it'll be entertaining."

She turned to leave, calling over her shoulder, "Come on, Pam. Let's go."

For a moment Pam looked from Allie to Dub without moving.

"*Pam*, come *on*."

Pam smiled uncertainly. "Okay, well, I'll see you guys."

"Bye, Pam," called Allie as Pam hurried away to catch up with Karen. She turned to Dub and said, "Wow. That was weird."

"Maybe Pam is a vertebrate, after all," mused Dub.

"Huh?"

"I just mean she showed a little backbone there for a minute."

Allie laughed. "Yeah. That was nice the way she stuck up for me."

"True," Dub agreed. "But let's not get carried away. We can't expect a leopard to change her spots overnight."

Allie laughed again. "Listen, I've got to talk to you about what happened today."

"What *did* happen today? What the heck were you

thinking of, saying you're going to interview the Snapping Turtle?"

"That's just it, Dub," Allie answered in a small voice. "I wasn't thinking. I didn't say it. I mean, I didn't mean to say it. It just came out."

Now it was Dub's turn to stop walking. "You mean—" His eyes grew big. "Like before?"

Allie nodded.

"Another ghost?" Dub asked in a hushed voice.

Allie shrugged. "I don't know. But it seemed . . . the same."

"It's so weird, Al. It's like you attract ghosts. Like you're some kind of—*ghost magnet.*"

"That's one way to put it, I guess," said Allie, not sure if the idea made her feel proud or uncomfortable. She recalled how confused and frightened she had been a few weeks earlier, when the ghost of Lucy Stiles had first appeared to her, asking for help. Compared to the way she'd felt then, she was relatively calm about the possibility that another ghost was contacting her. At least now she had some experience.

"Dub," she said slowly, thinking as she spoke. "I had a dream last night . . . about somebody who was trapped in a fire. It was sort of like the dream I had before, about Lucy Stiles falling from the cliff in Fossil Glen."

"Oh boy, here we go again," said Dub. "Let's see . . . Lucy's ghost came to you because she needed your help to prove she'd been murdered."

"Yeah. And now this ghost—"

"If it is a ghost," interjected Dub.

"—makes me blurt out Mrs. Hobbs's name."

Dub frowned. "So you're thinking the ghost, if that's what it is, wants you to discover something about Mrs. Hobbs."

Allie nodded.

"Maybe old Hobbling Hobbs killed somebody!" Dub exclaimed. "It wouldn't surprise me, actually."

"You know what's weird?" said Allie thoughtfully. "Just a little while ago I was messing around, saying there must be a reason why Mrs. Hobbs is so crabby and scary. I was kind of feeling sorry for her, imagining some great tragedy in her life. Maybe there *was* something . . . like a murder."

"Did you see the way she looked over at our lunch table today?" Dub asked with a shudder. "Like she knew we were talking about her."

"I'm glad I didn't," said Allie. It wasn't so much the things Mrs. Hobbs did that made her so scary, she reflected. It was the way she looked at you, hungrily, with her odd, beady eyes, that made you imagine all the awful things she *might* do.

"Well," Dub went on, "if this ghost wants you to

find out stuff about Hobbsy, having an excuse to interview her is pretty handy."

Allie brightened. "True. What a lucky break."

"Lucky for the ghost, maybe," Dub replied with a grin. "Not so lucky for you."

four

When Allie got home from school, she decided to take some shots at the lacrosse goal her dad had set up in the back yard. Her father would be home from work soon, after he picked up Michael at the baby-sitter's. Mr. Nichols had played lacrosse in college, and he'd bought both Allie and Michael sticks and started teaching them the basics.

Cradling the ball in the pocket of her stick the way her dad had shown her, she ran toward the goal and fired. Nothing happened. With disgust, she realized she'd let the stick drop too far in the back, and the ball had fallen out before she even took the shot.

She looked around the yard, relieved no one was there to see such a dumb display, and picked up the ball. After a few misses, she made a beautiful shot right in the corner of the net.

"And Nichols *scores*!" a voice boomed from the

window. "The rookie from Seneca, New York, has done it again, ladies and gentlemen!"

"Hi, Dad!" Allie called. "Come on out and play."

Soon she was joined by her father and Michael, who carried his own little stick, perfect for a four-year-old, and they played catch until Mrs. Nichols, too, came home from work and called them in to help with supper. Allie, her father, and Michael headed inside, laughing at Michael's last wild shot, which had gone over to the neighbors' yard and in the door of their doghouse.

At that moment, Allie heard the voice. It came from inside her head, and she knew from past experience that no one else could hear it. It was a male voice, not that of a kid or an old man, but somebody in between. There was an incredibly sad tone to it, and the sound caught midway in what Allie thought must be a sob.

"*A happy family, like yours. That's all I ever wanted. But* she *ruined everything.*"

Allie stopped dead in her tracks to listen, but there was nothing more. Her father and Michael were staring at her quizzically.

"You look funny," said Michael with a frown.

"Are you all right, Allie-Cat?" asked her father.

"Yeah. Yes. Really. I'm fine," Allie hastened to reassure him. What was she supposed to say? Oh, it's nothing, Dad. Just the voice of a ghost in my head.

She'd been able to explain her discovery of Lucy Stiles's murder to her parents and the police and reporters without mentioning that she'd been tipped off by Lucy's ghost. As she'd said to Dub, who would believe the truth, except him? She just didn't see the sense in worrying her parents over it, because worry they certainly would, even though she was perfectly fine and everything had worked out for the best.

She'd almost written the whole story in her journal for Mr. Henry to read: he'd asked her to, and she had the feeling he'd understand. But she'd chickened out at the last minute, fearing that teachers had to report crazy stuff kids said and did to the school psychologist. Then her parents would be called in, and they'd get all worried about her overactive imagination, the way they had before, and talk about having her "see someone."

The thing was, she didn't need a psychiatrist. But how could she tell her parents that, for some reason, she was a—what had Dub called her?—a ghost magnet?

She laughed as if nothing unusual had happened and said, "Everything's fine, you guys. Let's go eat."

"Let's eat! Let's eat! Let's eat!" cried Michael.

Allie's father touched her shoulder. "Okay, Allie-Cat. If you say so."

But after they'd eaten and she'd helped her mother with the dishes, Allie went into her father's study to call Dub. "Dub, I heard a voice. It wasn't Lucy. This was a guy, and older."

"What'd he say?"

Allie told him, and Dub whistled under his breath. "*She* ruined everything," he repeated. "Do you think *she* is Mrs. Hobbs?"

"I don't know," Allie said, although it was what she thought. The idea made her afraid, and she didn't want to get herself any more frightened of Mrs. Hobbs than she already was. "It could be anybody, I guess."

"Yeah," said Dub, but he didn't sound convinced. "You know, Al, maybe you should pick a different person to interview. Just say you changed your mind. It's no big deal, no matter what Karen says."

"Oh, I don't care about that," Allie said, even though Karen's taunts still stung. "I want to go through with it. Dub, he sounded so sad. He came to me for a reason. I wish I could remember everything we found out about ghosts on the Internet."

"Hang on. I bookmarked that page. I'm sitting right here by my computer. Let's see . . ."

Allie could hear him clicking away as he spoke. "Here it is. 'True ghost stories.' You want to hear it again?"

"Yes," said Allie, making a mental note to remember the name of the Web site. She'd gotten in the habit of relying on Dub's expertise on the Internet, but she meant to begin putting her own computer to better use.

Dub began to read: " 'In almost every case, the ghost is an unwilling spirit who was treated unfairly in life and who can find no rest until the wrongs against him or her are redressed. Some ghosts seek revenge, others seek justice. Some appear to the person who wronged them; others choose a person, often a stranger, whom they believe can make things right again. Then, and only then, can the spirit be at peace and leave the human world behind.' "

"And I'm the stranger he picked," said Allie. She could hear her own quick, excited breathing over the phone. "I wonder why."

"I don't know," said Dub. "But just because he chose you to help him do whatever he's got to do, it doesn't mean you have to go along with it. I mean, you don't *have* to take orders from a ghost." He paused. "Do you?"

"I don't think so." Allie thought for a minute and added, "No. Lucy didn't make me follow the clues that she gave me. I wanted to."

"Okay."

"And I want to help this guy, too, Dub. Whoever he is. The trouble is, all we have to go on is that stuff we read. Plus our experience with Lucy."

"*Our* experience?" Dub said.

"You know what I mean. Maybe it happened to

me, but— Well, I'd never have gotten through it without you."

There was an embarrassed silence on the phone.

"Okay, then," Dub said at last. "You're interviewing Mrs. Hobbs. Good. We'll just take this one step at a time. I'll see you tomorrow."

"Thanks, Dub. Bye," said Allie. She hung up, grateful that Dub had said *we*. At least she wasn't in this alone.

Whatever *this* was.

five

After math, Mr. Henry said, "Okay, let's take a minute for you all to tell me whom you've chosen for your interviews."

Joey raised his hand. "Are you going to bring Hoover in to hear our presentations?"

Twenty-five voices chorused, "Pleeeease, Mr. Henry!"

Hoover was Mr. Henry's golden retriever. Mr. Henry brought her to school quite often, and all the kids loved her. She never missed a field trip. She had been along on the class trip to Fossil Glen, and had even helped Allie to solve Lucy Stiles's murder.

Mr. Henry was smiling. "Good idea, Joey. Miss Hoover would never forgive me if she missed your grandfather's story of the *Hindenburg* disaster. If that's what you've decided on."

"It is," Joey assured him.

Mr. Henry continued around the room. Pam stuck with her aunt and Dub with his inventor friend. Brad announced that he was interviewing the "black sheep of his mother's family," his Uncle Hal. In a sullen voice Karen said she guessed she'd have to choose her grandmother. Julie Horwitz announced that she was conducting an e-mail conversation with a man who was living in a tent in Antarctica and studying penguins. Everyone was pretty impressed by that. Or at least they were until Allie repeated her intention to interview Mrs. Hobbs.

This time, a hush fell over the room. The silence was finally broken by Julie, who asked in a puzzled voice, "But *why*?"

Allie tried to think of an answer that would make sense to her classmates. "Well, I just think—" she began, and then her voice faltered. She tried again. "We've all known Mrs. Hobbs since kindergarten, but we don't really *know* her."

"I know all *I* need to know, thank you very much," said Karen.

There were a few chuckles at that, but Mr. Henry gave Karen his warning look, and the room quieted. "Go on, Allie," he said.

Allie continued in a small voice. "I guess I wonder about her. About her real life, outside the cafeteria, I mean."

Allie could feel Karen's scornful glare from across the room, but she kept her eyes straight ahead.

"But, Allie," said Julie, in the same puzzled, worried voice, "aren't you *scared*?"

Yes, thought Allie. But there's no way I'm going to admit it in front of Karen.

Mr. Henry saved her from answering. "Why would Allie be frightened of Mrs. Hobbs?" he asked.

There was a moment of silence, during which Allie imagined all the other kids were thinking the same thing she was. There was some stuff that every kid knew that grown-ups just didn't get. Mr. Henry was the coolest teacher in the whole school, but even he, it appeared, was clueless about the Snapping Turtle.

Joey tried to explain. " 'Cause she's *creepy*. I mean, all you have to do is look at her."

"You know better than to judge someone by her appearance, Joey. That's something we've been talking about all year."

"I know, Mr. Henry, but—" Joey glanced around the room for help.

Brad jumped in. "Maybe she doesn't do it to teachers, but when she looks at a kid, it's like she wants to eat you or suck your brains out or something."

Karen whispered sweetly, "If she's looking for brains, then I guess you don't have anything to worry about, Brad."

As usual, Allie noticed, Karen had made sure Mr. Henry didn't hear her.

"Mrs. Hobbs has been at this school longer than anybody else, and as far as I know, she hasn't eaten even one student," he said with a smile. "Allie, I think it's wonderful that you're going to interview her. Maybe you'll stop some of these crazy rumors. Did you know that Mrs. Hobbs was recently given a promotion?"

Allie shook her head. Promotion? To what? she wondered.

"She's already Head Hairnet," said Karen.

"She's always been in charge of our cafeteria," Mr. Henry corrected. "Now she's the cafeteria manager for the entire district. Maybe you can ask her about that, Allie, to help break the ice."

"Whoop-dee-doo," Karen muttered sarcastically. "I can't wait to hear all about the Snapping Turtle's big career move."

"Excuse me, Karen, what did you say?" asked Mr. Henry.

"Nothing," answered Karen with an innocent smile.

Mr. Henry turned to Allie. "Have you spoken to Mrs. Hobbs about the project yet?"

"No," said Allie, her heart speeding up at the mere thought of it.

Mr. Henry looked at his watch and said, "First

lunch hasn't started yet. This is probably a good time to catch her. Why don't you run down and check?"

Allie felt her mouth drop open. "*Now?*" she asked.

Mr. Henry nodded. "Sure. Go ahead." Then, oblivious to the effect of his suggestion on Allie, he continued around the room with his survey. "Wendy? Whom have you chosen to interview?"

Allie, meanwhile, was feeling something very close to panic. She'd known she was going to have to speak to Mrs. Hobbs at some point, but not *right then*. She felt completely unprepared. She glanced at Dub, who looked back with sympathy and mouthed the words "It'll be okay."

She wished she could raise her hand and ask if Dub could come along with her, but she knew how stupid that would look. Slowly, she rose from her seat and walked toward the door, her mind droning a dramatic narration: The condemned girl took what would turn out to be her final steps. Little did her teacher and classmates know they would never see her again . . .

In the hallway she tried to shrug off her dire thoughts and plan what she was going to say. She told herself she didn't have to actually do the interview; all she had to do was get Mrs. Hobbs to agree to it.

She walked down the long basement corridor and past the boiler room. Following the smell of sauerkraut, she reached the cafeteria, where one of the cafeteria ladies was dumping a big pot of steaming hot dogs onto a metal serving tray.

"Is Mrs. Hobbs here?" Allie asked.

The woman looked up, her face damp and pink from the steam, her expression astonished. "You want to see her?" she asked doubtfully.

Clearly, kids didn't often arrive at the cafeteria asking to see the boss.

Allie nodded. "Yes, please. Unless she's too busy," she added hopefully.

The woman jerked her head toward the kitchen, which lay beyond the serving counter. "Back there." She turned away to pick up another pot, mumbling something to herself. Allie didn't quite catch it, but it sounded like "Poor kid must be new here."

The long fluorescent lights on the kitchen ceiling buzzed and flickered unpleasantly, washing everything in the room in a sickly greenish tinge. Allie looked about uneasily, but there was no one in sight. She was feeling relieved until a huge metal door swung open. In the sudden blast of frigid air that poured from the walk-in freezer, Mrs. Hobbs appeared.

For a moment that seemed to last forever, Allie stood locked in the grip of Mrs. Hobbs's penetrating gaze. Briefly Allie thought that Mrs. Hobbs was staring over her shoulder, at something behind her. Allie turned to look, and the carton Mrs. Hobbs was holding fell to the floor with a sudden crash.

Allie dropped to her knees, desperate to escape those dark, narrowed eyes, and began gathering up scattered Popsicles. "I didn't mean to startle you!" she cried. "I came because I, I mean, my class—"

Mrs. Hobbs remained still and silent while Allie fumbled with the Popsicles and blundered through her explanation. "I'm Allie Nichols. I'm in Mr. Henry's class, and we're all supposed to interview somebody for Elders Day, and I wondered if it would be all right"—Allie gulped and forged ahead—"if I interviewed you."

She stood up, placed the box of Popsicles on the countertop, and forced herself to look directly at Mrs. Hobbs. Immediately she wished she hadn't. The woman was even more unsettling up close than from a safe distance away.

It wasn't her size that made her intimidating. She was only a little taller than Allie, neither fat nor skinny. Actually, Allie thought, from the neck down she looked pretty normal. Above the neck was another story. As Mr. Henry had said, Allie knew better than to judge people by the way they looked. On the other hand, she'd never seen anyone who looked like Mrs. Hobbs.

One red-rimmed eye drooped slightly lower than

the other, and in places the skin of her face and neck had an odd, stretched, shiny look. Her thin lips twitched, but she didn't utter a word. Her silence was even more disconcerting than her appearance.

Was she angry because of the spilled Popsicles? Did she enjoy frightening Allie with her naked glaring eyes and refusal to speak? Or did she always look and act this way? It was impossible to tell.

Allie had had all she could stand. She was about to flee when the woman spoke one low, guttural syllable.

"*Why?*"

In a shaking voice, Allie replied, "Excuse me?"

"*Why?*"

Allie heard the distrust and suspicion in Mrs. Hobbs's voice. She knew that what Mrs. Hobbs was really asking was "Why *me*?" She knew, too, that everything depended on the next words out of her mouth. Any mention of a ghost was out of the question, of course.

"Mr. Henry said you just got promoted, and I thought that was pretty good—" She had been about to say, "for an old person," but caught herself in time. "I thought you could tell me about that, maybe. And, well," she paused, and finished, "I think everyone has a story to tell, don't you?"

She looked down at the floor and held her breath,

waiting for Mrs. Hobbs's reaction. There was another long silence. Allie could feel the woman's eyes boring into her.

Then Mrs. Hobbs cleared her throat several times. In a voice that sounded as if it came from the back of a deep, empty cave, she said, "Tomorrow."

It took Allie a moment to comprehend what had happened. She looked up into that inscrutable face and whispered, "When?"

"Two o'clock."

Allie's mind raced. Mrs. Hobbs probably finished work at two, but school was still in session at that hour. She'd have to ask Mr. Henry to excuse her from class to do her interview. She thought it would be all right with him, but she wasn't sure. She certainly wasn't about to argue with Mrs. Hobbs, however.

So she nodded and turned to leave. At the door she stopped and added, "Thank you."

But Mrs. Hobbs was gone.

Allie ran from the cafeteria, feeling a chill that had nothing to do with the cold air from the cafeteria's walk-in freezer.

SIX

When Allie returned, Mr. Henry was talking to the class about Elders Day. "What are some effective questions you might ask the person you're interviewing?" he asked.

"How about 'When were you born?' " suggested Brad.

Pam shook her head. "It's rude to ask people how old they are," she proclaimed.

"Not in an interview. Right, Mr. Henry? Besides, we already know they're old or we wouldn't have picked 'em for Elders Day."

Mr. Henry looked around at the class. "What do the rest of you think?"

Finally it was decided that it was okay to ask, and if the person didn't want to answer, that was okay, too.

Mr. Henry added that he wasn't too concerned

about the actual age of the subjects. "I'd rather you choose someone you're interested in, regardless of age," he said. "Your parents are your elders, too, you know."

"That makes you an elder, too!" said Joey. "Good thing you have us to keep you young, huh, Mr. Henry?"

"I don't know what I'd do without you, Joey. Now, what else might you want to ask in your interview?"

"How about asking if there's a certain day or event they remember for some reason?" suggested Wendy.

"Great idea," Mr. Henry said.

As her classmates threw out other possible questions, Allie found her mind wandering. There was nothing she could do to stop it, even though she probably needed help more than anyone else in planning her interview. After her brief encounter with Mrs. Hobbs that morning, she was having a hard time even imagining how the conversation might go. Once she had asked about Mrs. Hobbs's promotion, what then?

"Mrs. Hobbs, all the students are scared to death of you. Rumor has it that you hate kids. Is this true?"

No.

"Mrs. Hobbs, a ghost made me pick you for my class project. Do you have any idea who it might be?"

No way.

"Mrs. Hobbs, your nickname is the Snapping Turtle. Would you care to comment?"

No, no, no.

"Allie?"

Startled, she looked up at Mr. Henry. "Earth to Allie," he said with a little smile. "Were you able to see Mrs. Hobbs?"

"Yes," she answered sheepishly.

"Did she agree to talk with you?"

"Yes. She wants me to come back at two o'clock tomorrow."

"Well, that's fine," said Mr. Henry. "You keep an eye on the clock tomorrow, and just leave when you need to."

"Okay. Thank you."

Allie's classmates were looking at her, their expressions showing sympathy mixed with relief that they were not in her shoes. All except for Karen, who smirked triumphantly at Allie's obvious unhappiness.

"Speaking of Mrs. Hobbs," said Mr. Henry, "it's time we headed down to the cafeteria."

Allie rose along with the others and got her lunch bag from her backpack. Mr. Henry caught her eye and said, "Allie, could I speak to you for a moment?"

As the class began walking down the hallway, Allie joined Mr. Henry at the end of the line.

"I was wondering if I could hire you this week-end," he said.

"Sure," Allie answered. "What do you want me to do?"

"Some friends and I got tickets to a Broadway show, so I'll be going to the city for the weekend. It was kind of a last-minute thing, and I need someone to take care of Hoover."

"I'll do it!" Allie said eagerly. "And you don't have to pay me!" She was enchanted by Mr. Henry's big, gentle golden retriever, and would have loved a dog of her own. Unfortunately, Michael was allergic to them. "But I can't keep her at my house."

"Oh, you won't have to," Mr. Henry assured her. "All I need you to do is stop over in the morning and again around dinnertime to feed her and check her water dish. Maybe play with her a little." He made a sad face and added, "She'll probably be pretty lonely."

"Poor Hoovey," said Allie. "Sure, I'd be glad to do it, Mr. Henry."

"She has a doggy door that goes from the house to her fenced-in yard, so she'll be able to get out any time she needs to. I'll leave the bag of food up on the counter to make sure she can't get into it."

"How much should I give her?"

"Two cups in the morning and one at night."

"Okay," said Allie. "But won't the house be locked? How will I get in?"

"Same way as Hoover," said Mr. Henry, his face absolutely straight. "Doggy door."

"Mr. Henry!"

"Okay, okay," he said, laughing. "I'll leave a key under the flowerpot to the right of the door."

"Gee, thanks," said Allie, smiling back at him.

"Thank *you*, Allie," he said. "It'll be a big load off my mind, knowing you're watching Hoover."

"Don't worry, Mr. Henry. I'll take good care of her."

"I know you will. Hey, can you tell me more about Mrs. Hobbs? How did things go?"

Allie hesitated. "All right, I guess," she said. "She doesn't seem to like me very much, though."

"She will, when she gets to know you," Mr. Henry said.

Allie wished she felt as sure about that as he did. At least, she reminded herself, Mrs. Hobbs *had* agreed to the interview. She could have said no. Maybe she hated kids, but hated Allie a little bit less than all the others.

When they reached the cafeteria, Mr. Henry left the class to go to the teachers' room, and Dub fell in beside Allie as they walked to their table. "Well," he said, "how bad was it?"

"The worst! First of all, she hardly talks at all. And when she does, *she sounds like this*." Allie spoke in a low croak in imitation of Mrs. Hobbs's creepy voice.

"Wow," said Dub, impressed. "But if she doesn't talk, it's going to be a tough interview."

"No kidding," replied Allie.

When they were seated at their usual table in the cafeteria, Allie found herself facing the lunch counter. She tried to avoid looking in that direction. But once, she glanced up and saw Mrs. Hobbs staring her way with a flat, penetrating gaze that took in everything and gave away nothing. Allie shivered and looked down at her hands.

"What am I going to say to her tomorrow?" Allie asked Dub. There was a touch of desperation in her voice.

"Weren't you listening in class just now?"

"Sort of."

"Well, you can ask when she was born," Dub said. "Then ask about her family—"

"Yeah," Karen chimed in from the other end of the table. "Ask if her mother was a snapping turtle and her father a warthog, or was it the other way around? And ask her if she auditioned for the movie *Bride of Frankenstein*." Karen's laughter rang through the cafeteria, and her face was flushed with pleasure at her own wit.

"Hilarious," muttered Allie.

"Oooh, looks like someone's got a secret admirer," Karen said then, pointing toward the cafeteria line. Before Allie could stop herself she looked up, and once again, her eyes met those of Mrs. Hobbs. She forced herself to turn away.

"Would you quit it, Karen," she said furiously. "Don't make her think we're talking about her."

"But we are," Karen said, acting innocent. "What's wrong with that? And tomorrow you'll be having a cozy little conversation with her all by yourself. Won't *that* be fun?"

Allie put the rest of her sandwich back in her lunch bag. For some reason, she didn't feel hungry anymore.

seven

All that afternoon and evening, and all through school the next day, Allie waited for a sign from her ghost. She hoped that soon he'd let her know what it was he wanted from her. Ghosts, she was learning, had their own ways of doing things. At the moment, she wished he'd give her some clues about how to get through her interview with Mrs. Hobbs.

At ten minutes to two she had just about given up, when the face of a young man appeared in her mind's eye. He was very handsome, with a shock of unruly black hair and large, dark, sorrowful eyes. Her heart began to beat rapidly, as she felt those eyes looking right into her soul. They seemed to be imploring her to do something. But what?

"Ask her about the fire."

It was the voice again—*his* voice, sad and pleading and filled with some terrible knowledge. It had come with a suggestion for the interview, just when she needed one.

Ask about the fire? The fire! Immediately Allie's dream came rushing back to her. She felt again the desperation of knowing there was someone behind the door, someone who would die unless she got there in time.

A horrible thought gripped her. Was that how *he* had died? Maybe *he* had been the one behind the door, the one who hadn't been saved. Her mind raced on, picturing it, and a sick feeling spread through the pit of her stomach.

A glance at the clock told her it was three minutes to two. Time to go. Filled with dread, she reached into her desk for her notebook and a pen, and rose from her seat. Mr. Henry looked at the clock. He gave her a brief nod and a smile as she left the room.

The cafeteria was deserted. Allie was accustomed to the usual hubbub that went on at lunchtime, and the utter silence was oddly disturbing. She stepped through the door to the kitchen. "Mrs. Hobbs?" Her voice quavered, and the words echoed back to her. She cleared her throat and called again. "Mrs. Hobbs?"

This time Mrs. Hobbs appeared from behind a bank of large coolers. She didn't speak but walked toward a small table and sat down. The table was covered with piles of papers and order forms. There was another chair pulled up to the table, but Mrs. Hobbs didn't offer it to Allie. She simply sat, looking down at her lap.

Allie had the crazy thought that Mrs. Hobbs looked like a kid who'd been sent to the principal's office, waiting to hear her punishment. But that was ridiculous. Allie was the one who had reason to be nervous, and Mrs. Hobbs wasn't helping her to relax one bit.

"Mrs. Hobbs?" she began tentatively. "Could I sit down? It'll be easier to take notes." She gestured toward the empty chair.

Allie wasn't sure, but she thought Mrs. Hobbs nodded her head slightly. Taking that as permission, Allie sat down. She'd rehearsed her opening remarks over and over in her head. Trying to keep her voice slow and steady, she briefly explained again that her assignment was to interview an interesting or special person for Elders Day and that she'd prepared a few questions. She flipped open her notebook to the short list of questions she'd managed to come up with and said, "Is it okay if I begin?"

Mrs. Hobbs might have nodded again, very slightly.

"Maybe we could start with your job here at school. I understand you were recently promoted." Allie sat back in her chair, pleased with this opening.

She had tried to make her voice smooth and soothing, like the voices of the reporters on TV, and thought she sounded quite professional.

Mrs. Hobbs just sat there without speaking. Was that mistrust Allie saw in her eyes? Apprehension, definitely. The woman's hands clenched and writhed fretfully, and Allie had the impression she might stand up and bolt from the room at any moment. Why, Allie wondered, did Mrs. Hobbs seem so nervous?

Please, just answer the question, Allie prayed silently. But then she realized with dismay that she hadn't actually asked a question. Her opening comments, designed to put Mrs. Hobbs at ease and get her to start talking, hung in the air. Mrs. Hobbs was staring at her, and as before, Allie had no idea what the woman might be thinking.

"So," she said, trying to sound upbeat, "what exactly is your new job?" There. A direct question.

There was a pause. Then Mrs. Hobbs cleared her throat and said in a low voice, "Cafeteria manager."

This was going to be harder than Allie had dreamed. She had never really thought before about the way a conversation required two people, with both of them making an effort. But, she reminded herself, this wasn't a conversation, it was an interview, and she was the one who had requested it. So she asked another question, one to which she already knew the answer, hoping it would get Mrs. Hobbs talking.

"So now you're in charge of the high-school cafeteria, too, not just ours?"

Mrs. Hobbs nodded.

Uh-oh. Allie could see that asking yes or no questions was not going to work. The subject of Mrs. Hobbs's promotion didn't seem to be going anywhere. Allie consulted her list.

"How old are you?" she tried. Then she added quickly, "You don't have to answer that question if you don't want to."

But Mrs. Hobbs spoke. In the same low, tentative voice, she said, "Forty-one."

Allie tried to hide her astonishment. Forty-one? But that wasn't very old. Allie's mother was forty-two! And Mrs. Hobbs looked twice as old as Mrs. Nichols! Allie must have heard wrong.

Carefully she repeated, "Forty-one?"

Mrs. Hobbs nodded.

Allie was amazed, and relieved that Mr. Henry had said people her parents' age qualified as elders. "Okay," she said, taking a deep breath and glancing down at her notepad.

The next question on her list was a safe, easy one that would be certain to get Mrs. Hobbs talking. "Can you tell me about your family?" Allie asked brightly. Most older people she knew loved talking about their families. Pretty soon, Allie figured, Mrs. Hobbs would be digging in her pocketbook for a photo album.

But Mrs. Hobbs's head snapped up at the question. Eyes glittering, she looked at Allie as if she'd been struck. Her mouth moved, but no words came out.

When she'd written that question, Allie had tried to imagine a Mr. Hobbs and little Hobbs children, but she'd been unable to picture them. Still, there *had* to be a Mr. Hobbs, she'd reasoned, or there wouldn't be a Mrs. Hobbs.

Yet here was the woman, staring at Allie as if she'd never heard the word "family" before. Things were turning out even worse than Allie had expected. Feeling quite unnerved by now, she tried to think of something to move the conversation along.

"A husband?" she asked quietly. "Children?"

Mrs. Hobbs appeared to be seized by strong emotion. Her hands clenched even tighter, and a queer expression passed over her face. It looked to Allie like a mixture of anger, pain, and—something else.

"No one," she said in a raw, strangled voice.

Silently Allie rebuked herself. Stupid, stupid, stupid! Everyone knew Mrs. Hobbs hated kids. What a dumb question to ask. She struggled to think of something to say to change the subject.

"Is there a certain day that stands out for some

reason, or an event that made a big impression on you?"

Mrs. Hobbs looked down, and Allie saw that her hands were trembling. She felt very confused, and frightened by the deep emotion she had somehow aroused in the woman. She considered excusing herself and calling off the interview altogether, and decided it was the only sensible thing to do. The next item on her list was "Ask about the fire." How could she suddenly come out with a question like that? It was hopeless.

She started to rise, intending to say, "Thank you for your time, Mrs. Hobbs. That's all the information I need."

But instead, she heard herself blurt, "Tell me about the fire."

At this, Mrs. Hobbs jerked forward in her chair. Her eyes narrowed as she stared at Allie with disbelief. She whispered slowly, "What did you say?" Then faster, furiously, her voice growing louder: "How dare you ask me that!"

Allie stood up quickly and began to back away in terror.

Mrs. Hobbs rose to her feet, too, her words a choking, strangled cry. "You! You!"

Allie, mesmerized by shock and fear, continued backing away.

Suddenly a thin trickle of smoke rose from a stack

of papers lying on the table between her and Mrs. Hobbs. Allie watched in horrified fascination as the smoke grew thicker. Then a flicker of flame appeared at the edges of the papers and grew until the entire pile was ablaze.

Allie looked up into Mrs. Hobbs's face, which was twisted with hatred. "Leave me alone," she said slowly, her voice filled with such loathing that Allie shuddered at the sound. "Haven't you done enough?"

The fire alarm began its loud, steady clanging, and Allie turned and ran for her life.

eight

Allie raced out the nearest exit. Soon she saw Mr. Henry waving to get her attention, and she joined the rest of her class. They stood on the lawn with the other teachers and students, watching the firemen swarm into the building.

After about fifteen minutes, the fire chief came out and spoke with Ms. Gillespie, the principal. He handed her a large bullhorn, which she used to make an announcement. "Boys and girls, may I have your attention, please," she called. "I'd like to commend you for exiting the building so quickly and quietly. Chief Rasmussen has assured me that the fire is now under control. However, since there are only about ten minutes until school is dismissed, we will not, I repeat *not*, be going back into the building today."

A cheer went up from the crowd, and Ms. Gillespie waited for it to die down before she continued. "School will be open as usual on Monday morning. Bus students, when your teacher dismisses you, please line up on the sidewalk by the bus loop and wait for your bus to arrive. Walkers, when your teacher dismisses you, you may go home. See you all on Monday morning."

A buzz of excited conversation burst from the groups of children and teachers gathered on the grass.

"Mr. Henry, can we go now?"

"Hey, Mr. Henry! This means we don't have any homework, right? All our books are inside!"

"But, Mr. Henry, my backpack's in there, and there's stuff in it I really *need*."

Allie's mind was still spinning from her meeting with Mrs. Hobbs, but she was aware of the uproar around her. Mr. Henry signaled for quiet, and she tried to focus on what he was saying.

"All right, you heard Ms. Gillespie. We can't go back in the building. I'm sorry, Karen, but you'll have to do without your backpack."

Karen pouted. "This really stinks. My new lip gloss and nail polish are in there."

"Gee, Karen, that's terrible," said Brad, pushing out his lips and making loud kissing noises. "How will you live through the weekend?"

"Shut up, Brad," said Karen, keeping her voice

low so Mr. Henry wouldn't hear. "As if anyone would ever want to kiss *you*."

Allie tried to tune Karen out. She was waiting to hear what Mr. Henry had to say about Elders Day.

"No homework," he began.

A cheer rose from the class.

"*Except*," he added with emphasis, "don't forget that Elders Day is Monday, and you'll need to have your presentations ready."

Allie raised her hand. "But, Mr. Henry, my interview with Mrs. Hobbs was interrupted by the fire drill."

"I don't imagine you'll be able to get in touch with Mrs. Hobbs over the weekend," said Mr. Henry thoughtfully. "Is there someone else you can choose instead?"

Allie felt a rush of relief. She was off the hook. Nobody could say she hadn't *tried* to interview Mrs. Hobbs.

"Looks like you were saved by the bell," Karen drawled sarcastically.

Allie ignored her. She supposed she could call her grandparents in North Carolina, and interview one of them. But what about her ghost, she wondered guiltily. He was counting on her. She only wished she knew why.

"I—I'll figure something out," she said at last.

"Atta girl," Mr. Henry answered approvingly.

Then he dismissed the bus students and, finally, the walkers.

Before she left, he said, "Hoover's looking forward to seeing you, Allie. I'll feed her before I leave today, so you won't have to come over until the morning. I'm not sure when I'll get home Sunday evening, though, so she'll need you to give her dinner."

"No problem, Mr. Henry," said Allie. "Have a fun trip, and don't worry about Hoover."

She ran to catch up with Dub, who was walking slowly, waiting for her. "Hey, Dub," she said urgently. "You won't believe—"

Just then, to Allie's surprise, Pam fell into step beside them and asked eagerly, "How did your interview go?"

"Yeah, Al," said Dub. "Was it okay?"

Allie was torn. She was dying to tell Dub the whole story, but she couldn't, not in front of Pam. Even though Pam was smiling in a friendly way and appeared genuinely interested, Allie felt wary. It wasn't very long ago that Pam had joined Karen in treating Allie as if she had cooties or something. Allie looked around to see if Karen, too, was nearby.

Pam seemed to read her mind. "Karen called her mother for a ride." She made a face. "I heard her say she was 'totally traumatized' by the fire and couldn't possibly walk home."

Dub snorted. Karen was the only kid in school,

the only kid Allie knew, who had her own cell phone. As far as Allie could tell, Karen used it mostly to order her mother to pick her up and take her places.

"For crying out loud," said Allie. "If anybody should be 'totally traumatized,' I should. The interview was unbelievably awful. Mrs. Hobbs scared me half to death. I was about to run out of there when the fire alarm rang."

"You really *were* saved by the bell!" said Pam, looking impressed.

"All the firemen headed for the cafeteria," said Dub. "Is that where the fire was?"

"I think so," Allie said carefully. That was what she wanted to talk to Dub about privately—the fire and how it had started. She tried to think of a way to change the subject. "But listen to this!"

Dub and Pam both turned toward her with eager expressions.

"How old do you think she is?" Allie asked them.

"Mrs. Hobbs?" Pam shrugged. "At least a hundred."

"It's hard to tell with turtles," said Dub. "They're *born* looking old."

Allie paused to allow the suspense to build, then said, "Forty-one."

"No way!" Dub exclaimed. "Come on, Al. If she told you that, she was pulling your leg."

"Yeah, like my mom," added Pam. "She's been thirty-nine forever."

Allie said, "I really think she was telling the truth."

"But forty-one? That's the same age as my parents," protested Dub. "And she looks way older than they do."

"I know," said Allie.

"Maybe that's what being mean and hateful does to a person," Pam said thoughtfully.

"Then I guess we know what Karen's going to look like someday soon," Dub said with a grin.

Allie laughed, then covered her mouth and looked quickly to see how Pam was reacting. To Allie's relief, Pam was trying to hide a smile of her own.

"What makes Karen act that way?" Allie asked, looking at Pam. It was something she'd always been curious about, and this seemed a good time to ask.

Pam said quietly, "Sometimes I think she's jealous."

"Of what?" Allie asked.

"Of everybody and everything. But especially you."

"*Me!*" Allie nearly choked with surprise. "Don't make me laugh. Why would she be jealous of *me*?"

Pam shrugged. " 'Cause cool stuff happens to you, like that whole thing in Fossil Glen. You were, like, a *hero*. And because Mr. Henry likes you, and so do the other kids."

"Wait a second," said Allie. "Karen's the popular one. All the kids like *her*."

Pam shook her head slowly. "It's more like they're scared of her. It's not the same thing."

Allie was so taken aback she could barely respond. She recognized a possible kernel of truth in what Pam had just said. But as for the rest . . . "Pam, come on. There's no way Karen is jealous of me. I am number one on her official 'loser' list. Ask anybody."

"And I'm number two," said Dub. "I consider it a badge of honor, actually."

"Me, too," said Allie, giving Dub a quick high-five.

"I wish I was as brave as you guys," Pam said wistfully. "I don't want to hang around with her anymore, but I don't know how to get out of it. I'm afraid of making her mad. No way I want to be her next victim."

"I don't blame you," Allie said sympathetically.

"Just don't let her get to you," Dub advised.

"Easy for you to say," said Pam. "But I'm going to try."

Allie, too, wished she could let Karen's remarks roll off her back the way Dub did. She tried. Sometimes it worked, but there were plenty of times when Karen still had the power to make her feel lousy.

When they reached Pam's street, she turned off to go home, saying, "See you guys later." Allie and Dub called goodbye, and finally, Allie was able to turn to Dub. "I've been dying to tell you this! Mrs. Hobbs started that fire!"

"What?" Dub's eyes grew round. "How?"

Allie stopped walking and held on to Dub's arm. "I don't know how. All I know is, my ghost said, 'Ask her about the fire,' and when I did, she got really mad. She was screaming at me and everything— and all of a sudden some papers on the table started to smoke, and then they burst into flames. There was nobody there but us, Dub. No matches, nothing. Just her and her creepy, crazy eyes."

"You're telling me she started the fire with her *eyes*?" Dub asked incredulously.

"I don't know," Allie answered. "But I saw it happen, Dub." Her voice shook as she remembered. "I can hardly believe it myself."

"Do you think she was trying to hurt you? Scare you? Or just get rid of you?"

"I don't know."

"Well, at least you have a perfect excuse for interviewing someone else," Dub said. "That's a relief."

"I guess," said Allie hesitantly.

"You don't sound so sure."

"I'm not," Allie said.

Dub stared at her as if she were a drooling lunatic. "Excuse me, but wasn't it you who just told me Mrs. Hobbs freaked out on you and scared you to death?"

"Well, yeah," she admitted.

Dub waited for her to explain.

"Believe me, I'd love to never see Mrs. Hobbs again . . ."

"But . . . ?" Dub prompted.

"But what about my ghost?"

"What about him?"

Eagerly Allie told Dub about the voice and the face appearing to her just before she went to the cafeteria. "He was so young, Dub. Like nineteen, or maybe twenty. Too young to die, anyway. And really cute."

Dub rolled his eyes.

"And so sad-looking," Allie went on. "So—" She stopped, fumbling for words to describe how the ghost had made her feel. He had aroused both her curiosity and her sympathy. More than that, though, he'd made her feel as if he needed her. "He seemed so sweet and—"

"So *dead*," Dub reminded her.

"Dub! Geez!" Allie snapped.

"Well, listen to yourself. You sound like you're in love with him or something."

Allie stopped walking and looked at Dub indignantly. "That's ridiculous and you know it. He was great, the way he helped me out just when I needed him."

"What do you think I've been trying to do?" asked

Dub quietly. When Allie didn't answer, he added, "Besides, what did he do to help you, anyway?"

"Right before two o'clock, when I was all worried about the interview, he gave me the words to say. That was when he told me to ask about the fire."

"Oh, that was great advice," said Dub sarcastically. "The interview really went smoothly after you said that."

"It's not his fault she flipped out!"

Dub shrugged.

"And it's not his fault he's dead! Dub, I think he died in a fire. And after what happened today in the cafeteria, I think Mrs. Hobbs had something to do with it. Why else would she get so upset when I mentioned it?"

"Well, maybe—" Dub began.

Allie interrupted. "Hey! I know! My ghost told me to ask about the fire, so he must want me to know something. But maybe I can find out without having to interview Mrs. Hobbs again! Remember how we looked in old newspapers to find information about Lucy's disappearance?"

Cautiously, Dub nodded.

"We could look up stuff about big fires and see if Mrs. Hobbs was involved."

"But we can't get into school to use the library," said Dub.

"So we'll go to the public library tomorrow."

"I thought we were going roller-blading tomorrow."

"Well, we were. But now we've got to do this."

"We've *got* to?" Dub repeated.

"Yes."

"Getting kind of bossy, aren't you?"

"Come on, Dub! It's for my ghost."

Dub gave her an odd look, then said, "Well, you can go to the library if you want. I'm going blading."

"But, Dub! I was counting on you to help me."

"I was trying to, Al. But you don't seem to be listening. Why don't you ask your boyfriend to help? He always seems to be there, right when you need him."

He turned off onto his street, leaving Allie with her mouth hanging open in astonishment.

nine

That evening at supper Allie told her parents that Mr. Henry had asked her to watch Hoover. "Can Michael come with me tomorrow?" she asked. "If he's over his allergies, we can get a dog!"

Her mother looked horrified. "No, you're not taking Michael!" she protested. "Of course he's still allergic. He'd itch and sniffle and sneeze and be miserable."

"Well, I just thought we could check—"

"Nice try, Al," her father said with a smile. "But I'm afraid Mike can't go. It's flattering, though, that Mr. Henry has so much faith in you, don't you think?"

"Yeah," said Allie proudly.

"Mr. Henry lives . . . where? Over on Highland Avenue?"

"Yeah. It's only five or six blocks. I'll just go over

on my bike." She added wistfully, "Are you sure there aren't pills Mike could take?"

"We've been through this, Al," Mrs. Nichols answered. Then, in what Allie thought was an obvious attempt to change the subject, her mother said, "I heard a lot of fire sirens this afternoon. Anybody know what happened?"

"The fire was at school," Allie answered. "It was kind of weird, actually. I was in the cafeteria interviewing Mrs. Hobbs—"

"The Snapping Turtle!" Michael shouted gleefully.

Allie had told her family about Mrs. Hobbs and the Elders Day project the night before. Michael had been entranced by Allie's description of the scary lady at the lunch counter. He'd spent the rest of the evening making believe he was a snapping turtle, ambushing Allie and her parents and pretending to bite them with his powerful jaws.

Allie groaned. "Don't start, Mikey," she warned. "Or I'll call the *real* Snapping Turtle and ask her to come over here and bite *you*."

Michael considered this. "Will not," he said. But he didn't sound too sure.

Allie continued her story, trying to decide how much of the truth to tell. She wished, not for the first time, that she could simply announce to her parents and to the world that ghosts were real and they'd better get used to it. But she couldn't do that, not unless she wanted her parents to start worrying and wondering if she was out of touch with reality, the way they had before. Could she tell about Mrs. Hobbs starting the fire? She decided to feel her parents out on the subject.

"So, anyway," she said, "the fire started in the cafeteria. We all had to leave the building, and we got out a little early because Ms. Gillespie didn't want us going back inside."

"Do they know how the fire started?" asked Allie's mother.

"No." Which was true. Only she and Mrs. Hobbs knew that. And Dub, of course.

Dub. What the heck was the matter with him, anyway? She pushed the thought from her mind. Whatever it was, she was sure he'd get over it.

"Did you ever hear of a fire starting all by itself?" Allie asked casually.

To her surprise, her father said, "Sure. Spontaneous combustion."

The words rang a bell, but Allie couldn't quite recall what they meant.

"Remember when Aunt Corky's house burned down?"

Allie nodded. "Oh yeah. The fire started in a plastic garbage can in the garage. They left a bunch of rags there that were soaked in something."

"Some sort of varnish," said Mrs. Nichols.

"Right. The rags warmed up in the sun, and that's all it takes. Spontaneous combustion."

But that wasn't what had happened in the cafeteria. "Have you ever heard of a person starting a fire with his *mind*?"

Mrs. Nichols looked skeptical, but Allie's father said, "There's a name for that. Telekinesis, I think. It means causing objects to move using the force of the mind, as you said. Maybe it would include starting fires. I don't think it's very scientific. It's associated more with parapsychology."

"What's that?" Allie asked.

"Oh, it has to do with séances, Ouija boards, and that kind of crackpot stuff."

Crackpot stuff, Allie thought. Like ghosts.

"I'm just glad you all got out safely," said Allie's mother. "Now, let's do a little planning for tomorrow. What are you all going to do while I'm slaving away at the store?"

Mrs. Nichols owned an antiques shop, which was open on Saturdays. Her weekend employee was sick, so she was going to have to work all day.

"I've got to mow the lawn," said Mr. Nichols, "and Mike and I are going to the high school lacrosse game. Allie-Cat, you're coming, too, right?"

"No, I have to go to the library to do some research."

"I thought you and Dub were going to try skating at the new rink," said Mrs. Nichols.

"Well, we were, but I've got to work on my project," said Allie. Thinking about Dub made her feel uneasy again. She decided to call him after dinner and make sure he was over whatever had been bugging him.

When she'd finished drying the dishes and putting them away, she dialed Dub's number. If he was mad about not going skating, she was ready to compromise. When he answered she said, "Hey, Dub? I was thinking maybe we could go to the library and then go skating."

There was silence at the other end of the line.

"Dub? You there?"

"Yeah. It's just that— Well, when you said you weren't going, I called some other people."

"Oh." Allie felt let down. "Who'd you call?"

"Brad and Joey, but they both had stuff to do. So I'm going with Pam."

Allie was stunned. "You called *Pam*?"

"Yeah."

"What happened to her being a—a leopard?"

"Come on, Al, she was acting pretty nice today, don't you think?"

Now it was Allie's turn to be silent. Dub was right, but that didn't mean she had to like it. In fact, she didn't at all like the way this conversation was making her feel. Dub was *her* friend. What was he doing going skating with Pam? Especially when she really needed him. "Yeah, sure," she replied finally. "Okay, well, I guess I'll be seeing you."

"Okay. Bye."

As soon as Allie hung up, she felt like calling back. She and Dub had always been so close they could practically read each other's minds. Now all of a sudden they were acting ridiculous. She picked up the phone, then put it back in the cradle. If Dub wanted to go skating with Pam, fine.

She was going to the library.

Because of a ghost.

Maybe she was a crackpot, after all.

ten

Later that evening, Allie was in her bedroom when Michael appeared at the door in his pajamas. He was clutching the Scorpion, his favorite Galactic Warriors action figure, and sucking his thumb. He looked at her, his eyes big and worried.

"What's up, Mike?"

Slowly, he removed his thumb from his mouth and said in a low voice, "Did you call her?"

"Who?" Allie asked.

Michael looked about fearfully before saying, "You know." When Allie shook her head, he whispered, "The Snapping Turtle."

"Oh, Mikey, *no*. Come here." Allie patted the bed beside her.

But Michael didn't move. "You *said*."

"Oh, Mike, I know, but I was only kidding, Squirt-Face. Honest. Come here."

Michael took a few slow steps toward Allie, then stopped.

She got off the bed and went over to kneel in front of him. "Mikey, listen to me. I was just fooling around. The Snapping Turtle isn't coming here. She doesn't know where we live. And I didn't call her, I promise. I don't even know her phone number."

Michael was still looking at her mistrustfully. She decided to try joking with him. "Besides, who ever heard of a turtle talking on the telephone?"

A little smile began at the corners of Michael's mouth, then stopped. " 'Cept she's not really a turtle. She's a mean, scary lady."

"That's right, Mike. She's not a turtle. But she's not really so mean and scary." The last part wasn't true, but Allie figured her fib was for a good cause. She decided to try changing the subject. "Hey, are you all ready for bed?"

Michael nodded.

"Teeth brushed?"

Another nod.

"Okay. Let's go get in your bed, and you can tell me about the Warriors' latest adventures. Last I remember, the good guys were fighting the bad guys at the fort, right?"

Michael's eyes lit up. "Right!" He raced down the hallway to his room, beckoning Allie to follow him.

Silently blessing the creator of Galactic Warriors, Allie prepared to listen to another installment of the never-ending saga that spun from Michael's imagination.

She tried hard to pay attention, but her mind was wandering. Suddenly, in the middle of a long, involved battle between Vulture-Breath and Greelior, Michael said, "Who's that?"

Coming out of her reverie, Allie thought guiltily that Michael was quizzing her to see if she'd been listening. She was thinking how to fake an answer when Michael said matter-of-factly, "He's gone now."

He continued with the tale of the battle, and fifteen minutes later, he was sound asleep.

Allie went to her room to read. She *tried* to read, but it was no good. Thoughts of Dub and Pam and Mrs. Hobbs and her ghost kept running through her mind, making reading impossible.

Poor Michael had been afraid she would call Mrs. Hobbs. She shouldn't have teased him, knowing the way his imagination worked. She had told him she didn't know the woman's phone number, which was true. But she could probably find out. And it couldn't hurt to do so, she thought.

Paging through the phone book downstairs, she looked under the letter *H*. There were seven listings for Hobbs. Three had men's names: Otis, Vincent, and Gerald. One was for Hobbs Tavern. Then there were three with initials: D.L., E.M., and P.

She dialed the number for D.L. and got a recorded message with the voice of a little kid. Definitely the wrong Hobbs. She tried E.M. The phone rang eight times, and she was about to hang up when a low, gravelly voice answered and said suspiciously, "Hello?"

It was the Snapping Turtle! Allie would have known that voice anywhere. Seconds passed, during which Allie tried to collect her thoughts and decide what to say.

"Who is this?" Mrs. Hobbs asked. Her voice was louder now, filled with anger.

Intimidated by Mrs. Hobbs's irate tone, Allie didn't answer.

"*You!*"

Allie froze.

Furious panting came from the other end of the line. "Why can't you leave me alone?"

There was a loud clunk, followed by the dial tone. Allie stood with the phone to her ear, stunned. How had Mrs. Hobbs known who was calling? And why was she so enraged?

Allie shook her head and put the phone down. She was about to close the phone book, when she thought to check the address. It was 1228 Armstrong

Street, just two and a half blocks away. Good thing Michael didn't know that.

She called good night to her parents, washed up, and got into bed. As soon as she closed her eyes, *he* was there. She knew he wasn't actually there, but she felt that she could reach out and touch his face. She *wanted* to touch his face: his melancholy expression made her long to comfort him. And then he smiled, and her heart twisted in a way she'd never known before.

"You're special, Allie," he said softly.

His words flowed through Allie like a warm current. Listening to him, she felt special.

"I know you're someone I can count on."

"I am."

"Then you'll help me?"

"I will," Allie said. "I promise."

His hand reached out, and she imagined its soft caress on her cheek. *"She promised me, too, Allie,"* he said sadly. *"But she broke her promise."*

"I'm not like that," Allie said.

"I know. But you won't let Dub stop you, will you?"

Startled, Allie asked, "What do you mean?"

"He's jealous of me. You know that, don't you?"

Allie didn't know what to make of this remark. Dub jealous? Of a ghost? It was crazy. "He won't stop me," she said firmly.

"I knew I was right to choose you."

Allie kept her eyes shut tight, not wanting to lose his image, but already it was starting to waver and blur.

"Who are you?" she whispered as the face faded away entirely.

"I was John Walker. Until she ruined my life."

eleven

Even though she'd spent most of the night thinking about her ghost, John Walker, Allie was up early the next morning. Knowing his name made her feel somehow closer to him, and more determined than ever to find out his connection to Mrs. Hobbs.

She had already dressed and was in the kitchen, finishing her cereal, when her mother came downstairs in her nightgown. "Morning, Mom," said Allie. "I'm about to go feed Hoover. Then I'm going to the library."

"Goodness, Al," her mother said sleepily. "You're awfully gung-ho this morning."

"Yup," said Allie, eager to be off. "So I'll see you later, okay?"

"Hang on, please. Give me a second to wake up and think. What time are you going to finish at the library?"

"I don't know."

"Well, check in with your dad when you do, okay? He and Mike will be home until the lacrosse game at one. If you don't finish up before then, why don't you meet them over at the high school."

"Okay."

"Or you could come help me at the store," her mother teased.

"Gee, thanks, Mom," said Allie with a smile. "That makes even homework sound like fun."

"What about lunch?" her mother asked, looking concerned.

Allie patted her pocket. "I've got money. If I get hungry, I can go to that little store across from the library and get a sandwich."

"Okay, sweetie. Give me a kiss."

Allie kissed her mother's cheek and ran through the back door into the garage to get her bike and helmet.

At Mr. Henry's house, she reached under the flowerpot for the key and let herself into the kitchen. "Hoover," she called eagerly. "Come here, girl."

From the other room she heard the click-click-click of toenails against the floor. Then Hoover's big, shaggy, golden head appeared.

"Hi, Hoovey," Allie crooned, sinking to her knees as she always did so that she could bury her face in the dog's soft, warm fur. "Do you want to play first or eat first?"

But instead of bounding over for a hug, as usual, Hoover had come to an abrupt halt in the doorway. A low growl rumbled deep in her throat. Then she burst into a series of high, sharp barks and began backing away from Allie with small, nervous steps.

"Hoover, what's the matter? It's *me*," Allie said.

Thinking that perhaps Hoover was upset by Mr. Henry's absence or confused by her own sudden presence, Allie remained on her knees, trying to make herself as non-threatening as possible. She coaxed in a gentle voice, "Hey, Hoovey, it's only me. I came to feed you, buddy. Would you like that? Want some food, Hoover? Hmmm?"

But the fur was up on Hoover's neck now, and she continued to alternate between deep growls and shrill, excited barks. Allie was completely bewildered. She tried for several minutes to settle Hoover down, and finally couldn't stand it any longer. The poor dog became more and more distraught, and Allie couldn't bear to watch her. Deeply puzzled and dismayed, she filled the water and food dishes, and after one last pleading attempt to get Hoover to play, she let herself out of the house.

Riding into town, she thought she remembered hearing somewhere that dogs were sensitive to supernatural beings. It might have been in a movie she'd seen. If that was true, Hoover could be reacting to the ghost of John Walker. Did that mean he was always hanging around her? No, that couldn't be it. She'd spent a lot of time with Hoover when Lucy Stiles's ghost was around, and the dog had been fine.

When she got to the library and tugged on the heavy wooden door, nothing happened. She tried again to open it, then looked up at the sign with the library's hours: SATURDAY 9:00 A.M. TO 5:00 P.M.

She looked at her watch. Eight-fifteen. What a stupid morning this was turning out to be. Sighing with frustration, she sat down on the steps and watched the meager Saturday-morning traffic going by. Her thoughts spun in the same circles as they had the night before, with the added worry of Hoover's odd behavior thrown in.

Meanwhile, what was she going to do for forty-five minutes?

Armstrong Street wasn't far away. There wasn't any reason why she couldn't ride there on her bike and see if she could find number 1228. Maybe Mrs. Hobbs would be outside, and they could strike up a casual, friendly conversation about John Walker.

Yeah, right.

The only way she was going to find out about Mrs. Hobbs was the library. Which wasn't open yet. In the meantime, she thought, it wouldn't hurt to check out Mrs. Hobbs's house.

The morning was quiet as Allie pedaled slowly along, checking house numbers. She didn't often come down Armstrong Street, and she looked about curiously. A woman in a bathrobe came out to pick up the newspaper. A small black dog raced beside Allie's bike, barking frantically for a while, before turning around and heading home.

What's with all the dogs this morning? Allie wondered. She decided this one was merely performing its doggy duty to protect its territory.

As she reached the 1100's, she noticed that the houses became smaller and closer together, and were often in need of paint or repair. Here and there she spotted a falling-down porch, a boarded-over window, a missing stair tread. Well-manicured flower beds and careful landscaping slowly gave way to weed-filled lawns and haphazard clumps of unpruned bushes and scraggly trees.

And then she was in front of number 1228. The yard was small and neatly kept, but it wasn't the yard that claimed Allie's attention. It was the house. It looked like two houses stuck together. The right side was perfectly normal. It was painted white, with black shutters at the curtained windows, and there was a little porch with a rocking chair by the door. The left side was a framework of scrap boards and plywood, covered by tarps and tattered plastic sheeting.

To Allie it looked decidedly strange, even spooky. She rode by slowly, trying to imagine the reason for the house's queer appearance. People ran out of money for home-improvement projects, she knew that. Until recently the desk in her bedroom had been a piece of plywood held up by cinder blocks. Her parents had been saving for a long time to build a family room onto their house, and her mother wanted to remodel the old-fashioned kitchen someday, when they had the money.

Maybe Mrs. Hobbs had been saving to fix up her house, too. Maybe her promotion would help. Or maybe she liked it that way, although Allie had never heard of anyone deliberately finishing just one side of a house.

At any rate, Allie had wanted to see where Mrs. Hobbs lived, and now she had done it. She took one last look back and thought she saw the curtain in the upper right window slip back into place, as though someone had been looking out.

Shrugging off the chill that tiptoed down her spine, she pedaled back to the library. When the doors opened at nine, she was the first person inside. Mrs. Harris, the librarian, explained to Allie that old editions of the local newspapers were stored on microfilm. She showed Allie how to thread the spool of film into a machine that made the tiny print readable.

Then she asked, "Now, what's the date of the paper you need?"

Allie was dumbfounded. "I don't know," she replied. "What I want to do is read about fires. Serious fires where somebody might have died."

She thought Mrs. Harris gave her a searching look before asking, "Recently?"

"No," said Allie. She racked her brain, trying to think of when the fire—if there had been a fire—might have taken place. "I guess I'd better go back twenty years or so," she said, feeling daunted by the prospect of looking through so many old newspapers.

But Mrs. Harris was smiling. "You're in luck," she said. "Several years ago we got a grant to create an index for *The Seneca Times*. It will tell us the days when items about fires appeared. But it would help if you could be even more specific. Do you have any other details that might focus the search so you don't have to look at every article about a fire?"

"I have a person's name," said Allie.

Mrs. Harris smiled. "Terrific. What is it?"

"Hobbs," said Allie.

"Hmmm. That rings a faint bell. Let's see . . ."

Using the index to find articles about fires that also mentioned the name Hobbs, Allie and Mrs. Harris worked quickly. They found several entries for

Hobbs that weren't about fires, and Allie said she wanted to see those articles as well. Soon she was seated at the microfilm reader browsing through old issues of *The Seneca Times*.

Some of the Hobbs articles were not about *her* Hobbs, but one, dated April 2, 1981, was an announcement of the March 30 marriage of Evelyn Murdoch and Clifford Hobbs. Allie realized she hadn't known Mrs. Hobbs's first name until now. The "E" in E. M. Hobbs was for Evelyn. It was such a pretty, feminine, *normal* name. Allie had trouble connecting it with the horrifying figure of Mrs. Hobbs.

Eagerly Allie read on. The wedding had been a private ceremony. No mention was made of ushers or bridesmaids or flowers, but there was a small, smudgy photograph of the newlyweds, and Allie studied it with fascination.

If she hadn't seen the accompanying words in black and white, she'd never have believed that the pretty young woman smiling into the camera was the feared cafeteria lady known as the Snapping Turtle. In a lace-collared dress with pearl earrings and a pearl necklace, Evelyn Hobbs was the picture of a blissful bride. One hand held a bouquet; the other was nestled in the hand of her husband. Clifford, while not dashingly handsome, appeared kind and cheerful and solid, and he was beaming at the camera with the look of a man who couldn't believe his good luck.

Allie spent a long time studying the photo, trying to reconcile that Mrs. Hobbs with the one she'd run from in terror the day before.

Finally, she moved on to the next article mentioning the name Evelyn Hobbs. In the October 2, 1981, edition of the paper, Allie came upon an announcement of the birth of Thomas Spencer Hobbs, son of Evelyn and Clifford Hobbs.

Her amazement then turned to horror as she read of the deaths of Clifford and Thomas Hobbs in a fire at their home at 1228 Armstrong Street on November 7, just a month after the baby's birth. Also dead from smoke inhalation was a visitor, John Walker.

As she read the name John Walker, a jolt of what felt almost like electricity passed through Allie's body. She had been right! John Walker, her ghost, *had* died in a fire. The same fire that had killed Mrs. Hobbs's husband and son.

With a mounting feeling of dread, Allie traced the story as it unfolded over the days that followed. The fire was under investigation. First, the fire chief said that the circumstances surrounding its origin were "suspicious." Upon further investigation, he announced that the fire had definitely been the work of an arsonist.

Mrs. Hobbs, mother and wife of two of the deceased, had been at a meeting of the women's auxiliary of her church at the time of the fire. Upon returning to find her house in flames, she had entered the burning building in an attempt to save her husband and infant. After receiving severe burns and suffering from smoke inhalation, she was rescued by firefighters.

The police had not announced the names of any suspects. However, the old newspaper stated, Mrs. Hobbs was continuing to be questioned at her room in the Seneca Heights Hospital.

Her hands trembling, Allie raced through the microfilmed pages to the next day's news. When she reached the first page of the November 9 edition, she eagerly began to scan it for an update of the fire investigation. Nothing on the first page . . . Nothing on the second . . . She was about to move to page 3 when the print began to dissolve.

Puzzled, she pushed the buttons to move the portion of the film that was under the lens. Immediately that began to dissolve as well. It looked as if it were melting right before her eyes. An acrid smell reached her nostrils, and a thin trickle of smoke rose from the microfilm reader. The film *was* melting! The smoke became thicker and started billowing from the machine.

Allie jumped up to find Mrs. Harris. But before she

was halfway across the room, a bell began to clang and the lights in the library flashed on and off. For the second time in two days, Allie found herself evacuating a smoky building with the sound of a fire alarm wailing in her ears.

twelve

With an odd sense of déjà vu, Allie watched as the fire trucks arrived and firemen swarmed the library. When they emerged shortly afterward, Allie sidled over to listen as Chief Rasmussen reported to Mrs. Harris.

"There was no actual fire," he said, "just lots of smoke. It appears there was a meltdown in that microfilm reader. Have you had trouble with it before?"

Mrs. Harris looked bewildered. "Never," she replied. "I can't imagine what could have happened. Those machines don't even get hot ordinarily." Just then she spotted Allie. "Oh, here's Allie Nichols, the young lady who was using it. Are you all right, dear?"

"I'm fine."

"Do you have any idea what happened?"

"No," said Allie. "All of a sudden the plastic started to melt and smoke like crazy. I jumped up to find you, but the alarm was already going off."

"Allie was doing research on local fires," Mrs. Harris explained to the chief. Then, with a startled laugh, she added, "What an odd coincidence!"

The chief raised his eyebrows and gave Allie a long, intent gaze. "What grade did you say you're in?" he asked finally.

I didn't say, Allie thought. Puzzled, she answered, "Sixth."

"So you must go to Seneca Heights School," the chief said thoughtfully.

She nodded, wondering what he was getting at.

"Were you there yesterday afternoon during the fire?"

Allie nodded again.

Mrs. Harris was looking back and forth from the chief to Allie with a baffled expression on her face. "There was a fire at the school, too?" she asked.

"Yes," said the chief, still looking speculatively at Allie. "And you say you came here to get information about fires, is that right?" he asked her.

"For a school project," she explained. Would that make the chief stop eyeing her with suspicion?

"Oh? Tell me about your project, Allie."

Now the chief must be thinking she was some kind of fire-setting weirdo. How was she supposed to explain herself? If she mentioned the ghost, he'd think she was a different kind of weirdo. For just a moment she wished she'd never heard the voice of her ghost, never seen his face. But no! She didn't really mean that. She simply needed to make the chief understand that she wasn't a firebug.

"The project is for Elders Day. We're supposed to interview somebody old, and I'm doing our cafeteria lady, Mrs. Hobbs."

The chief nodded. "I talked with her yesterday, after the fire at school."

"Oh," said Allie. "Well, I heard there was a fire in her past, too, so I was trying to find out about it. To get, you know, background information for the interview."

Chief Rasmussen nodded and said carefully, "I think we'd better talk about this with your parents, Allie."

"My *parents*? But *why*? If you'd just let me explain—"

"Are they at home?"

Allie felt like screaming. This was crazy, all of it: the fire at school, the fire in the library, and especially the idea that *she* had started them! Chief Rasmussen and Mrs. Harris were both looking at her warily.

She sighed and said, "My mom's at work. But Dad's home."

"Good," said the chief. "Let's go have a little chat

with him. Why don't you come on and ride with me?"

"I've got my bike." Allie pointed to the rack.

"Okay," the chief answered. "You go ahead and ride home, and I'll follow along after you. Where do you live?"

Allie gave him her address, and Chief Rasmussen snapped his fingers in recognition. "Allie Nichols! I thought you looked familiar. You're the girl who got rescued in Fossil Glen a few weeks ago, aren't you?"

Allie nodded.

The chief looked at her appraisingly. "And here you are again, right in the middle of the action."

Allie shrugged, thinking, You don't know the half of it.

As she mounted her bike, she heard the chief and Mrs. Harris talking in low tones. She couldn't quite catch the words, but she was sure they were talking about her, which made her nervous. She rode home in a daze, unable to believe what a mess the day was turning out to be.

When she pulled in the driveway, Michael was in the yard playing with his Galactic Warriors action figures. He looked up and saw her, and a cloud passed over his face. Standing up, hands on his hips, he shouted, "Liar!"

"Wh-what?"

"Liar, liar, big fat liar!"

"Mike," she said with exasperation, "what in the world are you talking about?"

Michael's face got the crumply look that meant he was trying not to cry. "You said she wouldn't come here, but she *did*. You said she's not really scary, but she *is*."

"She? Who?" Allie was so upset about Chief Rasmussen's imminent arrival that she was having a hard time making sense of what she was hearing. Suddenly her jaw dropped open. "You mean—?"

"The Snapping Turtle!" Michael cried, his chin wobbling. Then, bursting into tears, he wailed, "The Snapping Turtle came here, and she *is* scary, she *is*, she *is*, she *is*!"

thirteen

It was obvious to Allie that her father was more than a little surprised when she walked into the house with Chief Rasmussen. Mr. Nichols appeared completely bewildered by the chief's questions. No, there had never been a fire at their house. No, he'd never seen Allie playing with matches. No, as far as he knew, Allie had never started a fire; she even refused to light the gas grill, claiming she didn't like the sudden *whoosh* it made when it ignited. No, Allie had never shown any unusual interest whatsoever in fires of any kind.

"Would you mind telling me what this is all about?" he asked the chief at last.

Chief Rasmussen sighed. "I'm sorry to have bothered you," he said, including Allie in his apologetic glance. "It's my job to take note of any suspicious activity concerning fires, and I needed to satisfy myself that Allie here wasn't one of those kids whose fascination with fire leads them into trouble. If it's any consolation, I'm satisfied."

Whew, thought Allie.

"Well, that's a relief," said Mr. Nichols. "And there's no need to apologize. I'm grateful you're so conscientious."

"You know, I was new on the squad back when the Hobbs fire happened," the chief said, turning to Allie.

"Really?" she replied with interest. Maybe she'd find out the answers to some of her questions, after all. Not wanting to appear too eager, though, she waited.

"It was a real tragedy," he said, shaking his head at the memory. "You say you're interviewing Mrs. Hobbs for a project?"

"Yes," answered Allie.

"Then you should probably know this. Her husband and child died in that fire. Someone else, too, as I recall. I'm sure you don't want to bring up painful memories or ask her any awkward questions."

Too late for that, thought Allie. I already asked her about her family, and she got so mad she set fire to the cafeteria. She didn't say anything, though, hoping Chief Rasmussen would say more about the "someone else" who had died.

"The poor woman," said Allie's father, sounding horrified.

"Worst thing I've seen in all my years on the job," the chief said sadly.

"By the way," he added to Allie, "I'm sure glad you got out of the glen safely. According to the newspaper, you were quite the hero that day."

Allie smiled and shrugged, feeling embarrassed at the word "hero."

Her father and the chief talked for a few more moments. Then the chief left, saying again, "Sorry to have bothered you folks."

Allie was glad Chief Rasmussen had realized she wasn't a mentally deranged kid with a fire-starting fixation. But she knew her troubles were far from over.

Sure enough, her father turned to her with a look of exasperation. "Allie, what in Sam Hill is going on?"

It was one of her father's favorite expressions. Allie had often meant to ask him who Sam Hill was, anyway, but she didn't think this was the proper moment.

"First the cafeteria lady from your school, Mrs. Hobbs, comes here and scares Michael half to death, and next thing I know, the fire chief is here, asking questions as if he thinks you're a pyromaniac!"

Allie was still trying to take in the bizarre notion

that Mrs. Hobbs had actually come here, to her house.

"Dad, I have no idea what happened at the library. The microfilm just started to melt. It was really weird. Even Mrs. Harris said they've never had that problem before. And then, because there was a fire at school, too, and I happened to be in both places, the chief decided maybe I was some kind of creepy fire nut." She looked at her father beseechingly.

"Well, I think we got that straightened out," said Mr. Nichols. "At least, I hope so. But this visit from Mrs. Hobbs . . . Why do you think she came here? You haven't been bothering that poor woman, have you?"

Poor woman! Allie thought. "No!" she cried. "I asked if I could interview her and she said yes, only we got interrupted by the fire in the cafeteria. What was she doing here?"

Her father handed Allie a piece of folded paper. "When I told her you weren't home, she asked if she could leave a message."

"For me?" Allie asked with amazement.

Her father nodded, watching her curiously. Allie was curious, too, but mostly she felt bewildered and—yes, she admitted to herself—scared. She held the message gingerly between two fingertips, as if it were a poisonous snake or a ticking bomb. Feeling her father's eyes on her, she wished she could read it in the privacy of her room. But what excuse could she give for that?

Slowly, she unfolded the paper and gasped as she read the scribbled words:

Be careful.
You're playing with fire.

"What?" asked her father, his voice filled with concern. "Let me see that." He read the message and gave a low whistle. "What does she mean?"

"I don't know," Allie whispered, staring at the paper in horror.

"Allie," her father said, reaching out to touch her face, "you aren't 'playing with fire,' are you? First the chief, and now this . . ." His voice drifted off, and he lifted Allie's chin so he could look into her eyes.

Allie saw the worry there and said quickly, to reassure him, "No, Dad. Honest." She had a sudden urge to tell her father everything. He always tried to be fair. He tried to understand her. But asking him to understand about a ghost, and about her suspicions concerning Mrs. Hobbs, and about her reasons for looking up fires in the library—it was too much.

"Why would she write this?" he asked.

Allie shook her head, looking at the note as if it might yet reveal its meaning.

Mr. Nichols stood up. "Well, I don't like it. You

heard the chief. She's had a tough life. It could be she's mentally unbalanced." He thought for a moment and added, "I want you to stay away from her, Allie. Meanwhile, I think I should tell Chief Rasmussen about this note."

Allie put the note in her father's outstretched hand and watched while he looked up a number in the phone book and dialed. "Hello, this is Bill Nichols calling. I'd like to speak to Chief Rasmussen, please. Oh, he's not? Well, would you have him call me as soon as he comes in. It's important. Thank you."

Mr. Nichols gave their home phone number and hung up. Turning back to Allie, he said, "Are you okay, Allie-Cat?"

"Yeah, I guess."

Her father read the note again. "At first it sounds like a threat," he said slowly. "But if you read it a different way, it seems like a warning. Do you have any idea what the danger she's talking about might be?"

Allie shook her head. But she was thinking, Yes, *she's* the danger! She's telling me to stop trying to find out about her—or else.

Or else what? Allie wondered with a shiver.

"Well, threat or warning, it's a very peculiar thing to do, to leave a message like this for a kid." Mr. Nichols appeared to be thinking out loud as he said, "Especially for someone who works at the school.

You know, I think I'd better report this to Ms. Gillespie."

"You're going to tell the principal?" Allie said with surprise. Everything was happening so fast all of a sudden, and it felt way out of her control.

"I think she ought to know. In the meantime, stay away from Mrs. Hobbs."

"I was thinking I might still try to interview her for my project," Allie said hesitantly.

Her father looked at her in astonishment. "I think it's pretty evident that you need to find a new subject, don't you?"

"But I already told Mr. Henry and everybody I was interviewing Mrs. Hobbs," Allie protested.

"I'm sure Mr. Henry will understand."

Her father was right: Mr. Henry would understand. Besides, Allie had no idea how she'd go about finishing the interview, anyway, not to mention getting up the guts to do it. Still, she imagined Karen gloating with satisfaction: "I knew you'd never go through with it, Allie." Even worse was imagining the reaction of her ghost: "*I thought I could count on you, Allie. You promised you wouldn't let me down.*"

"Maybe I'm making too much of this," Mr. Nichols went on. "I certainly felt sorry for Mrs. Hobbs when I saw the way her face is scarred."

You wouldn't feel so sorry for her if you knew how she got those scars, Allie thought.

"But we have no way to know what's going on in her mind. Until we find out more, I want you to stay away from her."

"Okay, Dad," Allie said quietly.

"And give the subject of fires a rest, too, while you're at it, okay?" Mr. Nichols said with a touch of a smile.

"Okay." Allie tried to return his smile, but didn't feel as if she was very successful.

"I'm going to make that phone call now. Why don't you go find your brother and tell him that Mrs. Hobbs won't be coming back here anymore. The poor kid was scared out of his wits this morning."

"Okay."

"Tell him lunch will be ready soon."

Allie found Michael out in his "fort," a little shelter he'd made under a plastic table hidden deep within the forsythia bushes in a corner of the yard.

"Mike? Can I come in?"

There was a long silence. Finally, Michael said, "What's the password?"

Michael had created an elaborate password system based on the names of the good guys and bad guys in the Galactic Warriors universe.

"How should I know?"

"Guess."

Allie sighed. "Okay. Just give me a hint. Is it a good guy or a bad guy?"

"Bad guy."

"Vulture-Breath?"

"Wrong."

"Lady Stretcherly?"

"She's a *good* guy!"

Allie had no idea how Michael kept all this stuff straight. There were, it seemed to her, hundreds of characters, and Michael knew everything about each one of them. "Shark-Jaw?" she guessed, trying to hide her impatience.

"That was yesterday."

"*Michael.* Come on. I give up. Let me in."

"Guess one more time."

Exasperated, Allie racked her brain. "All right. Claw Girl?"

"Right."

Allie breathed a sigh of relief. She was pretty sure Michael changed the password whenever he felt like it, depending on his mood, but at least he had decided she was going to be allowed into the fort. On all fours she crawled in and sat down.

"Hi," she said.

Michael stared at her distrustfully from beneath lowered brows. "You said she wouldn't come here, and she did."

"I know, Mike. I'm sorry. Believe me, I had no idea she'd do that. Did she really frighten you?"

Michael nodded.

Allie was curious. "What did she do that was so scary?"

"She *looked* at me."

Allie waited. "She looked at you?" she repeated.

"Yeah," said Michael with a small sniffle. "And her eyes are scary. Like she has Superman vision. Like she sees inside you."

Allie shivered. So Michael felt Mrs. Hobbs's secret powers, too.

"And she looks scary."

"I know, Mike," Allie said. "But you don't have to worry. She's not going to hurt you."

"Promise?"

"Promise," Allie said, trying to sound certain. And why shouldn't she be? Mrs. Hobbs had done terrible things, yes, but she had no reason to harm Michael.

Michael sniffled again and asked, "How come she looks like that?"

"I don't know, Mike," Allie said. "But Dad says lunch will be ready soon." She wasn't about to tell a frightened four-year-old kid what she was sure was true: that Mrs. Hobbs had gotten burned in a fire she had set, a fire that had killed her own husband and child. Allie didn't want to believe it herself.

fourteen

Allie went inside and thought about the odd events of the morning, puzzling over the message from Mrs. Hobbs. Oh, how she longed to talk with Dub! She started to dial his number, then stopped. She reminded herself that Dub was skating with Pam. The traitor! Why was he acting so stupid, especially now?

He was the only person who knew that Allie saw and heard ghosts, the only person who had all the background information to advise her. Maybe he'd gotten home. She decided to call. To her relief, he answered.

"Dub? Hi. It's me." She stopped, unsure what to say next. She'd never before felt awkward with Dub. "Uh, I wasn't sure you'd be back. How was skating?"

"Great!"

"Oh."

"The new rink is *awesome*."

"Really?"

"Yeah."

"How's Pam?"

"She's really cool, Al, when you get to know her."

Allie couldn't believe her ears. She didn't want to believe her ears. She realized that what she was feeling was jealousy, which was totally dumb. How could she be jealous over Dub?

She remembered John Walker saying that Dub was jealous. Was it true? And was he trying to get back at Allie and make her feel the same way by hanging around with Pam? It was ridiculous! But maybe . . .

Meanwhile, Dub was going on and on. "Now that she's not really friends with Karen, she's completely different."

"Yeah, well, wasn't it you who said a leopard doesn't change her spots overnight?" Allie said.

"Geez, how come you're being so grouchy?"

"I'm *not* being grouchy!" Allie said loudly, hearing as she spoke how grouchy she sounded.

"If you say so," said Dub. "Hey, how was the library?"

"Something really, really strange happened." Allie took a deep breath and told him everything.

"Wow," Dub said when she had finished.

"I know. Pretty amazing how she made the microfilm melt, huh?"

"You think she did that?"

"Well, I don't think it was a coincidence. It happened just when I was reading that the fire was suspicious and they were questioning Mrs. Hobbs."

There was silence on the other end of the phone.

"Dub?"

"I'm here," Dub said slowly. "You know what you're saying, don't you? That would mean she killed her husband and her own baby."

"I know," said Allie. "And John Walker, too, don't forget. My ghost."

"But why would she go back in the house and nearly kill herself trying to save them if she set the fire in the first place?" Dub asked.

"To prevent anyone from suspecting her," Allie answered. To herself she added, Obviously.

"Sounds kind of far-fetched to me," Dub said matter-of-factly.

"Well, what do *you* think happened, then?" asked Allie, suddenly furious.

"I have no idea, Al," Dub said carefully. "I'm just saying it's kind of hard to believe that somebody would kill her own kid. Even the Snapping Turtle."

"Then why did she make the microfilm melt just when I was about to find out more? If she's innocent, why not let me read all about it in the paper?"

"I don't know." Dub was quiet for a minute. "But

if she can do stuff like that, maybe you should stay away from her."

"Yeah. But what about John Walker?"

"What about him?"

"Dub! What if I'd just ignored Lucy Stiles? Raymond Gagney would have gotten away with murdering her!"

"This seems different somehow."

"How?" Allie demanded.

"I don't know exactly," Dub said thoughtfully. "This guy Walker . . . I can't figure him out. If he really was murdered, and he wants you to prove it, he's not giving you much to go on. You know what I mean?"

Allie couldn't believe Dub. "What do you mean, *if* he was murdered?"

"Look, what I mean is, Lucy tried to help you, giving you clues and stuff," Dub went on. "This guy kind of shows up and looks sad, and leaves you to fill in the blanks by yourself."

Allie felt outraged on John Walker's behalf. The poor guy was dead, murdered, and all Dub could do was pick on him. "I'm sure he's trying his best," she said tightly.

"Maybe," said Dub. "But this letter from Hobbsy . . . It's creepy. I'm afraid you'll end up in trouble."

"Like I didn't end up in trouble last time, when Gag-Me was trying to kill me in the glen!"

"Okay, okay. All I'm saying is, you might not be so lucky this time, Al."

"Dub, since when are you such a wimp? I was hoping you'd help me figure out a plan."

"That's what I was trying to do," said Dub angrily. "But what do you need a wimp like me for? You've got your precious ghost, which is the only thing you seem to care about."

Allie listened with disbelief to the click of the phone as Dub hung up. Tears sprang to her eyes. It was so unfair! She'd always counted on Dub to understand, but he was just as bad as everyone else. No, worse. Because she'd thought she could count on him, no matter what.

"I'm sorry, Allie. It's awful when people you care about turn their backs on you, isn't it? I know how you feel."

He was there. His beautiful, sorrowful face appeared before her, his dark eyes looking into hers, his lips curved in a sympathetic smile. He knew how she felt. He was the only one who did.

"He's jealous, of course. But maybe he's right. Maybe you'd better stop. I don't want you to get hurt."

"Wait!" Allie cried. "Please don't disappear again. I don't want to give up, but I don't know how to go on. My dad says I have to stay away from Mrs. Hobbs."

103

"He's right."

"And let her get away with what she did to you? It isn't fair!"

"Life isn't fair," he said sadly. "And neither is death. But I shouldn't have asked you to take this on, Allie. The price is too high."

Allie was desperate to get some answers before John Walker disappeared again. "She killed you, didn't she?"

Walker's expression clouded. "Yes."

Allie gasped, although she had known the answer.

"You're amazing, Allie, to figure that out on your own. But you must stop now, to protect your sweet self from harm."

He reached out, and this time Allie was certain she could feel the caress of his hand on her cheek.

Then he was gone.

Allie put her hand to her face, trying to hold on to the feeling of John Walker's touch. How could she let him down, when she was all he had?

fifteen

Fired up with renewed determination, Allie dialed the phone number for the library, thinking that perhaps she could return and pick up her research where she'd left off. She got a recording saying that the library was closed for the rest of the day, Saturday, but would reopen on Sunday at noon. She sighed, frustrated by the delay.

The phone rang then, interrupting her fretting. She grabbed it quickly, allowing herself the small hope that it was Dub calling to make everything between them right again. "Hello?" she said eagerly.

"Allie?"

"Yes?"

"This is Chief Rasmussen."

"Oh," she said, surprised. "Hi. Do you want to talk to my dad?"

"Yes, I understand he called. But as long as I've got

you, let me tell you something. I got to thinking about the Hobbs fire, and I came back here to the station and looked up the old records. I thought you might be interested in what I found, if you're going to be interviewing Evelyn Hobbs."

Might be interested? She was dying to hear anything about Mrs. Hobbs and the fire that had killed John Walker! Trying to sound casual, she asked, "What did you find?"

"You'd have read about most of it in the newspaper, if the microfilm machine hadn't broken. But some of the details of the investigation didn't get into the papers. We had our suspicions, but we couldn't prove anything."

"Suspicions about what?"

"Well, we knew the fire was set deliberately."

"I read that you suspected it was," Allie answered eagerly. "Who did you think did it?"

At that moment a siren began to sound. Allie heard it over the phone line, incredibly shrill and loud, and in her other ear, more faintly, as it carried across town from the fire station.

Chief Rasmussen shouted over the sound, which must have been very loud to him, "That's the bell! Call me later!"

Allie sat for a moment, listening to the dial tone, then groaned and hung up.

Her father called up the stairs to say it was time

for lunch. As they were eating, Michael imitated the sound of the fire sirens that continued to blare across town, and Mr. Nichols asked, "Who was that on the phone?"

"It was Chief Rasmussen, but the fire alarm rang and he had to go."

"Poor guy's having a busy day," said Mr. Nichols.

Allie was glad her father didn't ask anything more. She didn't mention that the chief had information for her about Mrs. Hobbs.

Michael was blissfully trying to feed his grilled cheese sandwich to Vulture-Breath. "Can we go to the game now?" he asked.

"As soon as Vulture-Breath finishes his lunch," Mr. Nichols answered.

Ordinarily Allie loved watching lacrosse. But sitting in the high school bleachers next to Michael, she found it impossible to concentrate on the figures racing about on the field. Even when the Seneca Heights Hornets scored and Michael and her father rose to their feet, cheering excitedly, and the stands around her were going wild, Allie's thoughts were far from the game.

Either she had to figure out a way—and find the courage—to finish the interview with Mrs. Hobbs, or she had to pick somebody else. She didn't have much time: she had to make her presentation on Monday.

Her father and John Walker himself had both told

her to stay away from Mrs. Hobbs. Mrs. Hobbs had warned her off, and Dub had put in his two cents on the subject, as well. But Mrs. Hobbs was Allie's only link to John Walker. Mrs. Hobbs was the reason John Walker was stuck on earth as a ghost. Once the murder was exposed and justice was done, John Walker would be able to rest in peace, like Lucy Stiles. Everything led Allie to this same conclusion.

Her thoughts were interrupted by the sight of Dub walking by the bleachers with a hot dog in his hand. His face broke into a smile, and she rose from her seat to holler to him. She was about to open her mouth when she realized he wasn't looking her way. He began climbing the stands to join someone. Allie craned her neck to see who it was. A sick feeling washed through her as she watched Dub sit down next to Pam Wright. Pam playfully grabbed the hot dog, took a bite, and handed it back to Dub.

Allie could feel her face burning, and she quickly closed her mouth and looked away, trying to appear unconcerned. But it was too late: she'd been caught. To her dismay, her eyes fell on the smirking face of Karen Laver, sitting with her older brother and his cool friends several rows behind Allie and her family. Karen, who had obviously been watching the whole scene, gave Allie a pout of mock sympathy and mouthed the words "Poor baby" before breaking into a wide smile.

"Did you see that shot?" Allie's father shouted excitedly. "He faked the goalie right out of his shorts!"

Michael and Mr. Nichols exchanged a high-five to celebrate the score, and Michael shouted along with the crowd, "Go, Hornets! Sting 'em!"

Allie quickly turned away from Karen, furious with herself for revealing her feelings, and furious with Dub for making her look like a fool. She'd often wished that Pam would wise up and quit following Karen around like a loyal puppy dog. But now that Pam seemed to be doing just that, Allie felt angry at her, too.

Allie tried not to see the backs of Dub's and Pam's heads as they laughed and talked together in the bleachers below her, but her eyes kept being drawn in their direction. She hated them, and she hated the way she felt, but she couldn't stop herself.

sixteen

As Allie, Michael, and their father joined the crush of people leaving the lacrosse field after the game, they heard someone shouting loudly across the parking lot. A horrified murmur ran through the crowd, followed by a hush, then a burst of voices talking all at once.

"—a false alarm—"

"There wasn't any fire?"

"No. But Chief Rasmussen, he—"

"What happened?"

"There was an accident at the station house."

"An accident? Is he all right?"

"He fell."

"What did you say?" Without thinking, Allie grabbed the elbow of the man in front of her and spun him around to face her. "Tell me, please!"

The man was pale, his expression shocked. "They're

saying he—the chief—slipped. Off the pole, they say, when he was sliding down. They think he's hurt pretty badly."

Allie struggled to take in the man's words, feeling dizzy and unreal. No, that can't be true, she thought. He was at my house this morning. I just talked to him on the phone. It's impossible! There was something he wanted to tell me.

A sharp tingle ran through her, and she gasped, her hands flying to her mouth. Chief Rasmussen's fall had not been an accident!

A feeling of despair swept over her. Until now she had not understood the full extent of Mrs. Hobbs's power, or the depth of her malevolence. Even worse for Allie was the realization that whatever had happened to Chief Rasmussen was her fault. She was the one who had brought up the subject of the Hobbs fire, rekindling the chief's memories and causing him to look up the records on the case. He had been doing Allie a favor, trying to help with her project by giving her information from the investigation.

Allie felt her father's arms around her and heard his concerned voice. "Allie, honey, are you all right?" She buried her face in his chest and cried, while he patted her back and comforted her.

Allie wanted more than anything to pour out the whole story to her father, to pass the burden to him and let him decide what to do next. But she couldn't.

Mrs. Hobbs had hurt the chief because of his knowledge. Allie was afraid that if she told her father everything, he would be in danger, too. The idea of something happening to him terrified her.

Who else had she told about her suspicions?

Dub! Her heart lurched. Of course, Dub had pooh-poohed her, saying her theory was "far-fetched." She was mad at Dub, but she certainly didn't want anything to happen to him. She would have to be very, very careful from then on. She could confide in no one. Mrs. Hobbs had murdered three people and gotten away with it, then harmed another to protect her secret. There was no telling where she'd stop.

As these thoughts were racing through Allie's mind, her father lifted her tear-streaked face by the chin and looked sympathetically into her eyes. "Come on, Allie-Cat, let's go home." He kept one arm around her while they walked. Michael stayed close to her other side, and she felt his small hand grip hers when they crossed the grassy lawn of the high school.

"Don't be sad, Allie," he whispered. "It's okay."

It wasn't okay. Nothing was okay. But Michael didn't understand what was going on: he was just trying in his own way to make her feel better. Touched by his sweet concern, her eyes filled again with tears.

She wished she'd never told him anything about the Snapping Turtle. The less he knew about Mrs. Hobbs, the safer he'd be.

At home, Allie's father turned on the local TV news station, and they watched a report confirming Chief Rasmussen's accident at the station house shortly before noon that day. A representative from the hospital said that the chief had suffered a broken leg and a severe concussion. It was impossible to know how long he might remain unconscious.

Allie listened, terrified. Unconscious. Unable to tell what he knew. He'd been hurt, she was sure, because he'd been about to give Allie information Mrs. Hobbs didn't want her to have. It couldn't have been actual proof—he'd said that himself—or Mrs. Hobbs would be in jail. She must have covered her tracks very cleverly. Now she had acted to make sure they remained covered.

Several firemen were interviewed. None of them could understand how or why their chief had fallen.

"He could have slid down that pole with his eyes closed. It doesn't make sense," one said, before turning away from the camera.

"The false alarm makes it worse somehow," said another. "Chief always said it was his duty to give his life, if he had to, to save somebody from a fire. But this is just a waste." Then, angrily, he added, "Whoever called in that alarm oughta be ashamed."

Allie imagined Mrs. Hobbs listening, too, not ashamed at all, but gloating and triumphant.

Along with Allie's guilt and fear was the creepy feeling that Mrs. Hobbs somehow seemed to know what she was doing and thinking. I'm only a kid, she thought. How can I take on someone as powerful and treacherous as Mrs. Hobbs?

seventeen

During supper Allie picked at her meat loaf while her father and Michael told Mrs. Nichols all about what had happened when she was at work. Allie's mother shook her head in amazement and murmured, "I can hardly believe it. How terrible for the chief—for everybody involved."

"Do you think he'll be okay?" Allie asked.

"It's hard to tell with concussions," answered Mr. Nichols, "especially with adults. But there's a good chance he'll bounce back from this. Let's turn on the six-thirty news and see what they say."

He switched on the little TV set on the kitchen counter, and Allie cleared the table as they all listened. Soon a local reporter appeared, saying, "And now an update from County Hospital on the condition of Eric Rasmussen, fire chief for the town of Seneca."

The picture switched to a woman in a white lab coat, who was identified as Dr. Leslee Barness. "Chief Rasmussen is responding very well to therapy," she said. "He is healthy and strong, and he's a fighter. We expect rapid progress and a full recovery."

Allie, who had been holding her breath, let it out in a rush of relief.

"Oh, that's wonderful," said Mrs. Nichols.

"Good news, eh, Al?" said her dad.

Allie nodded, too grateful to speak. She began rinsing the dishes, praying silently that Mrs. Hobbs would leave the chief alone to get well. Allie hoped he would forget all about the Hobbs fire. She certainly wasn't going to ask him about it again, even if he recovered that very evening.

When the dishes were stacked in the dishwasher, she told her parents she was going to Mr. Henry's house to feed Hoover. She had an urge to ask one of them to come along with her, but told herself she was being a baby. After all, there was no reason for Mrs. Hobbs to care if she went to Mr. Henry's house. It was only seven o'clock and still light out, and Mr. Henry's house wasn't far away.

She gave her mother and father each a quick kiss on the cheek, saying, "I'll be back soon."

She grabbed her jacket from the hook by the

kitchen door, called goodbye, and ran for her bike. When she got to Mr. Henry's house, she checked the penned-in yard. There was no sign of Hoover outside, so she let herself into the kitchen, calling, "Hoover, it's suppertime!" She waited, listening, but heard nothing except the hum of the refrigerator and the tick of the clock on the wall.

"Hoooover," she crooned. "Come here, you good girl." She picked up a rubber squeak toy shaped like a bone and squeezed it a few times. "Want your bone, Hoovey? Want to play?" Ordinarily, Allie knew, when Hoover heard her squeak toy she came bounding from wherever she was, eager for a game of "chew the bone until it doesn't squeak anymore."

But there was no scramble of paws, no click of toenails against the floor, no sign of Hoover's big golden head at the kitchen door—nothing but an eerie silence. Allie stepped from the kitchen into the combination living-and-dining area and called, "Hoover?" Her voice came out sounding small and shaky. She cleared her throat and gave a hearty "Hoover?"

Allie's voice echoed in her ears, keeping time with the sudden loud thumping of her heart. She had allowed herself to hope that Hoover's odd behavior in the morning was a temporary aberration, and that the dog would be her old self by dinnertime. But where in the world could she be? If anything had happened to her, Allie would be responsible.

Uneasily Allie looked at the staircase that led to the second floor. She supposed she was going to have to go up there, but it didn't feel right to go traipsing around Mr. Henry's house. It felt like snooping. She had to look, though. What if Hoover was up there, sick or injured or— Taking a deep breath, she began climbing the stairs, calling the dog's name softly as she went.

At the top of the stairs was a bathroom. Allie glanced inside, but there was no sign of Hoover. To the right, she looked into a room that looked like an office, then into a spare bedroom. Nothing. She went back down the hallway and paused outside the doorway to what was clearly Mr. Henry's bedroom. She looked around, feeling very uncomfortable, almost guilty, about invading her teacher's privacy. There was no sign of Hoover, and she was about to go back downstairs when she heard a faint whimper.

"Hoover?" she whispered. "Is that you, girl?"

A series of low cries came from under the bed. Allie got down on her knees and crawled over, lifted the bedspread, and peered into the dim space. There, backed up against the wall as far from Allie as she could get, lay Hoover, trembling and whining in what appeared to be abject fear. This was so unlike the rambunctious dog Allie knew and loved, the dog Mr. Henry and all the kids at school loved, that Allie felt completely bewildered. Hoover, usually so jubilant and playful, was acting like an entirely different dog.

"Hoover," Allie pleaded, "what's the matter, girl?"

The dog, already pressed against the wall, tried to back even farther away. When she couldn't, she stiffened and let out a fierce, sharp bark. Then she curled her lips and bared her teeth, and a low growl came from deep inside.

Allie was terrified. She couldn't believe what was happening. She had no idea what she might have done to cause Hoover to act this way. All she knew was that she had to get away. Hoover was frightened and cornered, and even the gentlest dog might bite under those circumstances. Very slowly and deliberately, she backed away from the bed and inched, still backward, toward the door. She was afraid to stand up, afraid the movement would upset the dog further, afraid, too, of those jaws and teeth emerging from under the bed to close around her leg.

When she reached the door of the bedroom, she got quickly to her feet, slammed the door, and raced down the stairs to the kitchen. She stood for a moment, her heart pounding, while tears sprang to her eyes. She brushed them away, still unable to believe what had happened, unable to believe that she was frightened of the most sweet-natured dog she had ever known. It was equally strange and incredible, she thought, that Hoover appeared to be frightened of her.

With hands that were still trembling, Allie filled Hoover's food and water dishes and let herself out of the house. She stood for a moment, looking up at the second-floor windows as if they might give her some kind of explanation for what had happened inside, but they stared blankly back, revealing nothing.

She raced home, where her mother was reading to Michael. She explained to her father what had happened and how she had left Hoover in the bedroom with the door closed. Together, they got in the car and went back to Mr. Henry's house.

In the kitchen Mr. Nichols said, "You stay here, Al. I'll go up."

Allie listened to his footsteps ascend the stairs and cross the floor to Mr. Henry's room. She heard the door open and her father's muffled voice softly calling Hoover's name. Then, to her astonishment, her father said jovially, "Well, hello, Hoover, old girl! How are you, big puppy? You okay now, girl? You gave Allie quite a scare, you know. Come on downstairs. That's it, come on. Your supper's waiting. Oh yes, what a good girl."

Allie listened, amazed, as her father and Hoover came downstairs. Hoover bounded into the kitchen, her ears eagerly perked, her tail wagging happily. But before Allie could open her mouth, Hoover's entire demeanor changed. Her tail went between her legs, her ears flattened against her head, and her legs stiffened as she came abruptly to a halt. Then she huddled behind Mr. Nichols's legs, alternately whimpering and barking in short, sharp bursts.

"Dad!" Allie wailed. "What's wrong with her?"

"I don't know, Al," he said, looking baffled. "She was fine until—"

"Until she saw *me*!" Allie cried. "But, Dad, I didn't do anything to her, honest! Why is she acting like that? Why is she scared of me?"

"You didn't do anything, Allie. She's confused for some reason. Who knows why? Listen, why don't you wait in the car? I'll get her settled down, see if I can get her to eat something, and then we'll go."

Dejectedly, Allie went out and sat in the car. She had always credited animals, especially dogs, especially Hoover, with having a natural sense about people. Dogs seemed to know instinctively who was good and who was bad, who deserved their loyalty and love, and who didn't. It made Allie feel awful to have Hoover act as if she were the worst bad guy in the entire Galactic Warriors universe.

She'd been rejected by her best friend. Now she'd been spurned by a dog. The only person outside her family who really cared about her was a ghost. The memory of John Walker's sympathetic smile helped to soothe the aching place in Allie's heart.

eighteen

It took Allie a long time to get to sleep. Her brain felt like a blender, with terrible thoughts whirling round and round inside. Then, to her surprise, it was eight o'clock in the morning. She must have slept, after all.

She got out of bed and padded downstairs to the kitchen, where she fixed herself a bowl of cereal. She would have liked some company other than her own depressing thoughts, but the rest of the family slept late on Sundays.

Finally, her parents came down. Her mother began mixing pancake batter, and her father sat beside her at the table and said, "Would you like me to go over and check on Hoover this morning, Allie-Cat?"

"I guess so, Dad," Allie said glumly. "I don't want to torture her by making her see *me* again."

"Cheer up," said her dad. "When Mr. Henry gets home, I'm sure she'll start acting normal again."

"I hope you're right," said Allie, trying to smile back at her father.

"I think I'll run over there now, then. I'll be back for the final batch of pancakes."

"Okay, Dad. Thanks."

The phone began to ring as Mr. Nichols pulled the front door shut behind him. Allie answered, "Hello?"

"This is Alarm Services. Is Mrs. Ann Nichols there?"

"Just a minute, please."

Allie listened while her mother spoke quickly, then hung up.

"The alarm went off over at the store," Mrs. Nichols said, pushing her hair, still mussed from sleep, from her forehead. "I must have punched in the wrong code or something when I closed up last night. Usually Joan or Reggie sets it, but I was alone yesterday, in a hurry, as usual . . ." Mrs. Nichols was talking, sort of to Allie and sort of to herself, as she threw her raincoat on over her nightgown.

"I have to run down there, sweetie, just for a second. The batter's all ready. Would you like to start a batch of pancakes for you and Michael?"

"Sure."

"You'll have to wake him up. Be careful with that hot frying pan. I'll be back in two seconds."

"Okay, Mom."

Allie put some butter in the pan, waited for it to sizzle, and spread it evenly around. Michael liked lots of silver dollar pancakes, so she carefully spooned small dollops of batter until she had made twelve little circles. When the tops bubbled and the sides looked firm, she flipped them over and was happy to see that they looked perfect. Making perfect pancakes wasn't exactly a major accomplishment, but it still felt good to be doing *something* right.

Allie turned down the flame and called up the stairs to wake Michael. When he didn't answer, she ran to his room and found that he must have gotten up, after all.

"Michael?" She moved through the house, calling to him, but he didn't reply. Then, figuring that he must have gone out to his fort, she leaned out the kitchen door and called across the yard, "Michael! Your pancakes are ready!"

There was no answer. "Come on, Mike, quit fooling around! I made your favorites, and they're ready right now!"

No sound or movement came from the forsythia bushes. "Michael!" Allie said. "Give me a break!"

Michael still didn't answer.

"I'll eat them all myself," she threatened.

Silence.

"Darn you, Michael," she said angrily, storming across the lawn. The grass was still soaked with dew, and her slippers got wet, making her even madder. "Don't think for one minute I'm going to guess some stupid password to get you to come out of there," she grumbled, bending down and peering into the bushes.

There was no sign of Michael. Allie felt a peculiar mixture of exasperation and fear. "Michael!" she shouted. "Come out here right now, I'm not kidding!"

"I'm going to tell Mom and Dad," she added desperately when Michael didn't answer. "They're going to be home any minute, and they'll be really mad."

The yard was still and silent in the early-morning sun, except for the chirping of the birds. Allie raced back inside and ran through the house again, calling for Michael and checking every room. In his bedroom she looked under the bed, under the covers, and in the closet to make sure he wasn't hiding.

Finally, she let the truth wash over her. *Michael was gone.*

And she knew who had taken him.

In a near frenzy of panic, Allie tried to decide what to do. The idea of going after Michael by herself made her mouth feel cottony with fear. But waiting for her mother or father to come home would mean wasting precious minutes. An image of Michael, alone with the Snapping Turtle, hysterical with fear, filled her mind and nearly paralyzed her. No! She couldn't wait while the seconds ticked away, not while Michael was in danger.

A horrible thought took her breath away. Mrs. Hobbs must have known Mr. Nichols was out, and had caused the alarm to go off, summoning Allie's mother away, as well. Who knew what she might do to keep Allie's parents from returning?

Choking back a sob, Allie made up her mind. Quickly she threw a pair of jeans over her shorty pajama bottoms, pulled on some sneakers, and ran downstairs and out the front door. Then she flew to the garage, onto her bike, and out into the street, grateful that she didn't have far to go.

The street was deserted in the Sunday morning quiet. She stopped at 1228 Armstrong Street, got off her bike, and stashed it in the bushes. As Allie crept across the grass, her heart pounded under her pajama top. When she reached the steps that led up to the half of the porch that remained, a sudden noise made her gasp out loud and whirl around in terror. It was only one of the tarps that covered the roof and walls, flapping in a passing breeze.

On the porch she slipped quietly past the front door and over to the open window. She peered through the screen, terrified of what she might see. Her imagination offered images of Michael tied to a chair, blindfolded and gagged, choking on his sobs. It took her eyes a moment to adjust to the dim gloom of Mrs. Hobbs's living room. What she saw then caused her to gasp in disbelief.

nineteen

Mrs. Hobbs was sitting alone on a couch, weeping. There was no sign of Michael.

Allie was so stunned by the sight of the Snapping Turtle crying that for a moment she simply stood staring, watching the rise and fall of Mrs. Hobbs's shaking shoulders and listening to the lost, hopeless sounds of her sobs. Appalled, Allie wondered what in the world could have happened to make a woman like Mrs. Hobbs cry.

An answer too terrible to contemplate occurred to her. Had Mrs. Hobbs done something so awful to Michael that even she was feeling remorse? That thought put steel in Allie's spine. Without knocking, she burst into Mrs. Hobbs's living room. Having planned nothing—not what she was going to do or what she was going to say—she stood in the open doorway, her eyes locked furiously on the figure of Mrs. Hobbs.

Mrs. Hobbs lifted her tear-stained face. Her expression registered no surprise at Allie's intrusion, no anger, no emotion at all except a profound weariness. In a low, dull whisper, she said, "I give up."

Allie felt confused. Give up? Did Mrs. Hobbs mean she was giving Michael back? "Where is he?" Allie said, her voice sounding huge and angry in the tiny room.

Mrs. Hobbs's expression didn't change. "You know that as well as I do," she said tiredly. Her voice was as strange and gravelly as it had been in the cafeteria, only now there was no fury left in it.

Is she joking around with me? Allie wondered in amazement. "You didn't hurt him, did you?" she cried, taking a step toward the woman, feeling as if she might grab her and shake the answers out of her.

Mrs. Hobbs looked off toward the distance, to somewhere only she could see. "I suppose he thinks I did," she said quietly.

"No," Allie moaned, unable to bear the thought. "What did you do to him?"

"It doesn't matter anymore. I'm going to put an end to it once and for all."

Allie's mind was racing in frantic circles. Put an end to *what*? Michael's life? "Oh, please," Allie whimpered. "Please, no."

"I do wish you'd tell me something," Mrs. Hobbs went on. Her voice remained slow and monotonous, and her face still showed a complete absence of feeling. "How did he get you to play his twisted little game?"

Game? Allie shivered in the warm, stuffy room, chilled by the thought that Mrs. Hobbs must be mad. In that case, what was the best course of action? Should Allie force her way past the woman and search the house for Michael? No, she thought, she shouldn't do anything to make Mrs. Hobbs angry or upset. At the moment the woman was calm and unthreatening. Talk to her, Allie thought. Get her talking about Michael and maybe she'll tell you where he is.

She had asked about Michael's game. What game was she talking about? Allie racked her brain for an answer. "You mean the games he plays with those little plastic figures?" she asked desperately.

Mrs. Hobbs's dull expression changed momentarily to confusion. Then she moved her hand as if to wave away Allie's words and said, "Did you think he was nice? Did he flatter you? Did he turn those dark, soulful eyes on you and make your heart swell with sympathy? Did he make you believe he was the only person in the world who understood your feelings? Did he make you feel *needed*?"

It dawned on Allie that Mrs. Hobbs wasn't talking

about Michael at all. At the same time, the woman's odd questions settled uncomfortably in the back of Allie's mind, ringing a familiar bell. But she couldn't think about it then. *"Where is my brother?"* she screamed. *"What did you do to Michael?"*

Mrs. Hobbs merely stared at her dumbly, as if *Allie* was the one who was asking crazy questions.

Then Allie heard a small, plaintive voice wail, "Allie?"

"Michael!" Relief spread through her like warm butter, making her legs weak. She turned away from Mrs. Hobbs and shouted, "Michael, where *are* you?"

"Allie?" he said again. The sound came from somewhere outside, and Allie ran out onto the porch.

"It's me, Mike," she said urgently. "Keep talking so I can find you."

"I don't like this fort, Allie. I want to go home."

Allie followed Michael's voice to the unfinished side of the house. Was he under there somewhere? Trying to make herself sound calm and reassuring, she said, "Good idea, Mike. Let's go home. Come on out here and we'll go."

"I'm scared. It's dark."

Allie's heart wrenched at the pitiful sound of his voice. It was coming from somewhere under the part of the house that was covered with plywood and tarpaper and tarps. She lifted the edge of the plastic.

"Mike?"

When she heard sniffling and soft crying, she ripped the tarp from the staples that held it down and got to her knees. Only a small amount of light reached under the makeshift wall, but it was enough for her to see Michael's small, huddled form. She reached out to him, saying, "It's okay now, Squirt-Face. Come on. Let's go home."

Michael wriggled across the dirt and into Allie's arms, and for a moment they simply sat and hugged each other. Allie thought she had never been so happy in her entire life, and she squeezed her eyes shut and wept with relief.

Then she looked up and remembered where they were. She didn't want Michael frightened any more than he already was, so she brushed her tears away. Trying to make it seem like a game, she said as calmly as she could, "Okay, Mike. Let's run, okay? Ready? Come on!"

They ran across the grass, and Allie grabbed her bike from its hiding place in the bushes. She got on, lifted Michael onto the seat in front of her, and pushed off, pedaling furiously. As she turned off Armstrong Street, she looked back, half expecting to see Mrs. Hobbs lurching after them with her lopsided gait. But the street was empty.

When she reached Cumberland Road, Michael pointed excitedly to a fire truck and two police cars whose lights were flashing in front of their house.

What now? Allie wondered. She pulled into the driveway, and Mrs. Nichols burst out the front door. Her face, blotchy and swollen from crying, crumpled with relief, and she crushed Allie and Michael in a long, fierce embrace. "Thank God you're safe."

Inside, the house seemed filled with men and women in uniform. There was a period of confusion as the firefighters, their job completed, prepared to leave. It seemed everyone was talking at once. Allie heard the word "pancakes" and groaned. She had run out, leaving the heat on under the frying pan. Sorry as she was that Chief Rasmussen was in the hospital, Allie couldn't help feeling relieved that he hadn't witnessed this latest disaster. She imagined the panic her parents had felt upon returning home to find the pancakes burning, the smoke alarm blaring, and both their children missing.

Now Allie and Michael, their parents, and one remaining police officer were gathered in the living room. Michael was snuggled in his mother's arms, and Allie stood next to her father, his arm around her shoulder. Everyone was looking at her.

"What on earth were you thinking, running off like that?" asked Mrs. Nichols.

Allie could hear in her mother's voice that relief was giving way to anger. Now that Allie and Michael were safe and sound, they were going to have some explaining to do. Quickly Allie told how she'd been unable to find Michael to give him his breakfast and had gone to look for him.

Mr. and Mrs. Nichols turned to Mike. "Why did you run away, Mike? Where did you go?" asked Mr. Nichols.

Michael buried his face against his mother's chest and murmured something.

"What, honey? Tell Mommy and Daddy where you went."

Michael mumbled something else, and Allie caught the word "fort."

"Where was the fort? How did you get there?" Mrs. Nichols asked.

Allie couldn't hear Michael's muffled answer. She saw the policeman lean forward, trying to listen, too. Then she watched her mother turn pale. "The man took you?" Mrs. Nichols said, looking with alarm at Allie's father. "What man?"

Allie saw the fear in her mother's face and felt it spreading through her own stomach. She watched as her mother, struggling to keep the hysteria from her voice, gently pried Michael's head from her chest and looked him square in the eyes.

"He was a nice man, Mommy," Michael said.

Allie could tell her mother was trying to sound calm, but there was a tremor in her voice as she said, "Tell Mommy about the nice man. What was his name?"

Michael shrugged.

"Where did you see him?"

"In my room."

"This morning?" Mrs. Nichols asked incredulously.

Michael nodded. "When I woke up. He was there before. Remember, Allie?"

Allie, bewildered, shook her head. Her mother asked urgently, "Mike, did he talk to you?"

Another nod.

"What did he say?"

"He said he had a big fort. He said Allie was there, and I should come, too."

Allie stiffened at the idea that the man had used her name to gain Michael's trust. Mike's story was getting more and more peculiar.

"And so you went with him?"

Nod.

"In a car?"

Michael shook his head.

"You walked?"

Michael nodded.

"Allie," said her father. "Where was it that you found him?"

"On Armstrong Street. Under Mrs. Hobbs's house."

Her parents both looked completely baffled. "How did you ever think to go there?" asked her mother.

Allie didn't know how to answer. "I don't know. A

lucky hunch, I guess." She glanced toward the policeman, who was looking at her with a curious expression.

"Wait a minute," said her father. "He was at *Mrs. Hobbs's* house? She came here yesterday with that strange message, and today Michael ends up under her house? That can't be a coincidence. And I told you to stay away from her, Allie. I don't understand what made you go there."

"I don't either, really," Allie said. It was way too complicated to explain. "I just—"

She was saved by Michael. Eyes wide and fearful, he asked, "Was it the Snapping Turtle's fort?" His chin wobbled, and Allie's heart wobbled, too, in sympathy.

"No," she answered hurriedly. There was no point in making this worse for Michael than it had been.

"Did the man say anything to you about Mrs. Hobbs?" asked Mr. Nichols.

Michael shook his head.

"Did you see Mrs. Hobbs?"

"No."

Allie saw her parents look at each other, then turn toward the policeman and shrug in dismay. She knew that later there would be more questions.

Meanwhile, she tried to think things through. Michael said he had walked with the man to Mrs. Hobbs's house, which was possible, she supposed, since it was only two and a half blocks away. But how had the man gotten into Michael's bedroom in the early morning? How had he known about Michael's fascination with forts? How had he known to use Allie's name? And why had he taken Michael to Mrs. Hobbs's house, of all places?

Her mother was saying, "Bill? Do you suppose he was dreaming? Sleepwalking?"

"I was wondering the same thing," her father said slowly. "There couldn't really have been a man in his room."

"Was the house locked?" asked the policeman.

Mr. Nichols nodded. "I lock up tight every night. It doesn't make any sense . . ."

But to Allie it was beginning to make a horrible kind of sense. There was one man who could have come to Michael's bedroom even when the house was locked up tight, who knew all about Allie, and all about Mrs. Hobbs: John Walker.

Michael had said, "He was there before. Remember, Allie?" And now Allie did remember: it was Friday night, when she'd been in Michael's room, listening to his bedtime stories. "Who's that?" he'd asked. But before Allie could figure out what he was talking about, he'd said calmly, "He's gone now." And Allie had thought no more about it.

"Mike," she said softly, "what did the man look like?"

Michael frowned with concentration. "Funny," he said finally.

"He looked funny? How?"

Michael slipped his thumb into his mouth and talked around it. "Just funny."

Allie could imagine how John Walker had looked to Michael, his form wispy and insubstantial, yet undeniably real, and how Mike would not have the words to describe what he had seen.

Mrs. Hobbs's question came back to Allie: "Did you think he was *nice*?"

A "nice" man had appeared to Michael that morning, and Michael had gone trustingly with him to the "big fort."

Like a punch in the stomach, the realization came to Allie: She wasn't the only one in the family who could see ghosts.

twenty

Allie's brain was reeling. *Why* had Walker taken Michael? To protect him? From whom? Mrs. Hobbs? But then why take him to her house? Unless he thought that was the last place she'd look for him.

Although her mind was elsewhere, she was aware of the discussions going on around her as her parents and the police officer tried to figure out what had happened that morning. They kept coming back to the idea that Michael must have dreamed the nice man and had "followed" him out of the house while sleepwalking. It was the only explanation, they told one another, but it was hardly reassuring.

The policeman finally left, saying that they should call if they had any other thoughts or leads. Michael had fallen asleep in his mother's arms, his thumb in his mouth. Mrs. Nichols, looking worried, stroked his cheek tenderly.

"Bill," she said, "I think we should call Dr. Waheed about this sleepwalking business. It scares me to death to think what might have happened."

"Good idea."

While her parents spoke with Michael's pediatrician, Allie went into the family room to think. What had happened scared her to death, too. Michael didn't seem to be overly upset by his experience, but that was because he was too young to understand the danger he had been in. Why, she wondered over and over, would John Walker lure Michael to Mrs. Hobbs's house? It didn't make any more sense than the sight of Mrs. Hobbs weeping, or the weird things she had said. Allie felt lost, as if she understood nothing, and terribly alone.

She needed help.

She needed Dub.

She'd call him and— No. She couldn't call. It seemed that everything she said and did was seen and heard by Mrs. Hobbs, with her creepy powers, or by John Walker's ghost. And she didn't want either of them to know what she was doing until *she* knew what she was doing.

The screen saver on the family computer flashed its changing design at her, giving her an idea. She went over, logged on, and checked her buddy list. There was a smiley face next to Dub's name, "Cyberhead," indicating that he was online.

Cautiously, Allie clicked the "instant message" box and began to type:

DUB

She paused, not knowing how to begin. She longed for the old familiar ease she and Dub used to share, but she didn't know how to get it back. She wanted to make things right again, not just because she needed Dub's help, but because she missed him. She knew she had hurt Dub's feelings and made him angry. He'd made her mad, too. But at the moment, it was difficult to remember exactly what the problem had been.

DUB, IT'S ME. I AM SO, SO SORRY FOR BEING A JERK.

She clicked the Send button and waited nervously. She pictured Dub sitting at his computer, and the surprise on his face when her message popped up on his screen. She imagined him reading it, thinking, and . . . Too much time was going by. Dub wasn't going to reply.

She was about to give up when the little bell tinkled, and Dub's reply appeared in the instant message window.

MORE INFORMATION, PLEASE.

Oh boy, thought Allie. Dub wasn't going to make this easy. She thought for a minute, then typed again.

I THINK THIS WHOLE GHOST THING IS
MAKING ME CRAZY. I UNDERSTAND IF YOU LIKE
PAM BETTER NOW, BUT I'D RATHER HAVE YOU
FOR A FRIEND THAN ANYBODY (EVEN IF I
HAVEN'T BEEN ACTING LIKE IT).

She read it over and added one more thing before pushing Send.

IT'S POSSIBLE YOU WERE RIGHT ABOUT SOME
THINGS AND I WAS DUMB.

There. Dub would like that: he enjoyed being right about things. And he usually *was*, though ordinarily she wouldn't admit it, especially to him. But at the moment Allie was willing to flatter Dub like crazy if she had to. Besides, she really meant what she'd written.

TELL ME MORE ABOUT HOW DUMB YOU ARE.

Allie smiled to herself. She could feel Dub loosening up.

INDESCRIBABLY DUMB. DUMB AS A DODO.
DUMBER THAN DIRT.

That ought to satisfy him!

THAT'S IT? YOU AREN'T GOING TO GROVEL AT
MY FEET, BEGGING FOR FORGIVENESS? I VANT
TO SEE YOU SQVIRM, LIKE THE VORM YOU ARE.

Allie laughed out loud. That sounded like the old
Dub Whitwell talking! He was doing his famous impression of "General Vitvell."

I VILL DO ANYTHING YOU VANT, HERR
VITVELL. BEG, GROVEL, SQVIRM—LATER. RIGHT
NOW I REALLY NEED YOUR HELP.

OF COURSE YOU DO. PROCEED. BUT DO NOT
THINK YOU ARE FORGIVEN.

Allie felt her muscles relax, and realized how
tensely she'd been waiting for Dub to open the door
even a tiny crack. She began to type quickly.

THERE IS SOMETHING STRANGE GOING ON
WITH JOHN WALKER. I'M ONLINE INSTEAD OF
CALLING BECAUSE I'M HOPING THAT HE'S NOT
CLUED INTO COMPUTERS SINCE HE DIED 17
YEARS AGO. I COULD BE WRONG. HE MIGHT BE
READING THIS NOW. ANYWAY, I NEED YOU TO
GET INFO ABOUT HIM AT THE LIBRARY. YOU
KNOW WHAT HAPPENED WHEN I WENT THERE
YESTERDAY. CAN YOU GO?

There was a pause that was long enough to make
Allie nervous.

OKAY. WHAT DO I DO?

Allie breathed a deep sigh of relief, then typed,

CHECK SENECA TIMES NEWSPAPER INDEX
1975–1982 FOR ITEMS ON WALKER. COPY
ANYTHING INTERESTING.

GOT IT. I'LL COME OVER WHEN I'M DONE.

Allie's eyes filled with grateful tears as she typed:

THANKS, DUB. YOU'RE THE BEST.

SINCE WHEN? ☺

The instant message box showed that Dub had signed off. She wondered, too late, if it would be a mistake for him to come over with the information he found. There was no way to know—until it happened. She felt as if she were playing a game without knowing the rules.

Allie was thinking that, even though she seemed to attract them, she actually knew very little about ghosts. She'd had just one experience before. Having only that to go on, she'd assumed something similar was happening with John Walker.

But John Walker was turning out to be far more puzzling than Lucy Stiles had been. She didn't understand what he had done to Michael, and it made her uneasy. It was one thing for Walker to visit *her*, she thought. She was almost twelve and could handle it. Or, at least, she'd thought she could, up until now. But Michael was four!

In a weird way, she realized she wasn't surprised that Michael might have the same attraction for ghosts that she had. He'd always been open to all sorts of crazy possibilities, like trees that walked into his bedroom at night and little plastic creatures that held a universe of good and evil. He'd always been empathetic, too, seeming to know when Allie was upset, and trying, in his four year-old way, to cheer her up. So it wasn't too hard to imagine that John

Walker, after finding Allie so helpful, might try to enlist Michael in his quest.

But what was his quest? Allie had thought she knew, but now she was anything but sure. Whatever it was, she didn't want Michael mixed up in it.

Where did a ghost like Walker hang out, anyway? Where was he at that very moment, for instance? It was disconcerting, downright creepy even, not knowing when he might appear—or when he might be watching. If he had been murdered and wanted her to avenge him, why didn't he help her out? Why didn't he come to her and explain what was going on?

And then there was the whole matter of Mrs. Hobbs and her bizarre behavior that morning. The disturbing image of her crying alone in her living room came back to Allie.

Okay, she told herself. This is getting you nowhere. She thought about the sign that hung in the library at school: INFORMATION IS POWER. Dub was finding out what he could. While she waited, she could do the same.

She typed in the address of the Web site she and Dub had checked out before: www.trueghoststories. com. Maybe she'd learn something new, or else find a link to another helpful site.

She scrolled down through all the stories, which

were fascinating, but weren't what she was looking for. Somewhere, she recalled, there had been a kind of summary of all the articles, with conclusions drawn from the different examples. Ah! There.

> Many of the stories suggest that the strength and ability of a ghost are related to the age and power of the person at the time of his or her death. The ghost of an infant, therefore, is often said to be weak and ineffectual, making its presence known only by the faint sound of its cries. The ghost of a forty-year-old woman, on the other hand, may be able to make itself known to humans in many different ways in order to influence earthly events.

"Hmmmm," Allie thought out loud, "so Walker's ghost is probably stronger than Lucy's was." She read on:

> A ghost has unfinished business to complete before it can rest. It may wish to impart an important message, something it neglected to say while living. It may wish to warn, punish, or protect someone. Victims of murder, suicides, and people killed suddenly or violently most often have reason to return as ghosts.

Allie read with interest. This whole business was more complicated than she had thought. A ghost might possess many possible motives for coming back, not all of them necessarily good. She had been foolish, she realized, to assume that John Walker's story was similar to Lucy's or that his motives were the same. People were all different; why wouldn't their ghosts be, as well?

Lucy had been a nice kid who'd been murdered by a greedy slimeball. Her ghost had gone away once her murderer had been exposed.

Allie had figured that John Walker had also been harmed, and maybe he had. But suppose John Walker was a very different kind of ghost? Suppose he was returning for some reason other than justice? Suppose he was seeking revenge?

Or, Allie wondered further, what if a person had been mean, or really and truly crazy, in life? Would he come back as a mean, crazy ghost? What if his "unfinished business" was something evil or nasty?

What would make him go away?

These were questions that had never before occurred to Allie. She kept reading, looking for answers.

Ghosts can be put to rest by various techniques, some of them religious, some not.

Sometimes the ghost is satisfied when his unfinished business is completed, or when certain events have occurred to end his quest.

Various techniques? Certain events? That's real helpful, Allie thought irritably. She clicked on several links to other pages, but didn't find anything new or exciting. She was about to give up when she came across an interesting article written by an anthropologist who had interviewed hundreds of people claiming to have encountered a ghost.

So we see that most of the time the ghost is an unwilling spirit who longs to finish its business and rest. In these cases, if a particular requirement is met, the ghost is satisfied and is content to leave the human world behind.

However, those spirits whose nature could be characterized as essentially evil or vengeful may never be satisfied. They believe themselves to have been wronged so severely that they wish to continually punish the perceived wrongdoer(s).

Such a ghost must be either endured or laid to rest by the living.

Allie scrolled down, looking for some details about this "laying to rest" business. But there the article ended. She was staring at the screen in frustration when her mother called up the stairs to say that Dub had arrived.

She flew to the front door, anxious to hear what he had learned. As soon as she saw his flushed cheeks and eager expression, she knew that he'd found something juicy.

twenty-one

Allie put a finger to her lips, reminding Dub not to say anything that Walker could "overhear," and beckoned him into the family room. She pulled up a chair for Dub, sat down herself, and typed: SO WHAT DID YOU FIND?

Dub, wiggling his eyebrows tantalizingly, typed: ARE YOU READY FOR THIS?

In an agony of curiosity, Allie replied: JUST TELL!!

Dub handed her a piece of paper on which he'd copied the information he'd found. Allie read, "*The Seneca Times*, December 28, 1980: Evelyn Murdoch and John Walker announced their engagement. Evelyn, an employee of—"

She gasped loudly in disbelief. Dub looked at her and quickly typed: WHAT? YOU HAVEN'T GOTTEN TO THE GOOD PART.

ARE YOU KIDDING?! EVELYN MURDOCH IS MRS. HOBBS!

Dub's eyebrows lifted in amazement, and Allie realized she'd never told him that. SHE WAS EVELYN MURDOCH BEFORE SHE GOT MARRIED. I CAN'T BELIEVE SHE WAS ENGAGED TO JOHN WALKER!

Allie thought back, then wrote: SHE WAS ENGAGED TO WALKER IN DECEMBER AND MARRIED MR. HOBBS ON MARCH 30. THAT'S ONLY—she had to stop and calculate—THREE MONTHS LATER. WHAT HAPPENED???

Dub shrugged and pointed to the paper, urging Allie to continue reading.

The article went on to say that Evelyn Murdoch was employed by the school system and John Walker was the owner of Walker Motors, an auto repair shop. An April wedding was planned.

Allie looked up at Dub and mouthed the word "So?"

Dub held up his finger, signaling Allie to wait, while he juggled the rest of the papers in his hand. He found what he was looking for, but instead of handing it to Allie right away, he paused for dramatic effect.

She grabbed the paper and read that, on January 15, Walker Motors had burned to the ground. She looked at Dub and whispered, "No way!"

Dub nodded excitedly, and gestured for her to

keep reading his hastily scribbled notes. She learned that the fire had definitely been set on purpose and that the main, in fact the *only*, suspect had been John Walker.

Allie was barely able to breathe.

Dub typed: SOUNDS LIKE WALKER WAS EITHER A LOUSY CAR MECHANIC OR A LOUSY BUSINESSMAN. EITHER WAY, WALKER MOTORS WAS ABOUT TO GO BANKRUPT. SO WALKER BURNED IT DOWN TO COLLECT THE INSURANCE MONEY.

LET ME GUESS, Allie typed eagerly. THEY KNEW HE DID IT, BUT THEY COULDN'T PROVE IT.

Dub nodded, and Allie typed: JUST LIKE THE FIRE THAT KILLED MR. HOBBS AND THE BABY.

For a minute, neither of them moved.

BUT WALKER DIED IN THAT SECOND FIRE, Dub wrote. WHY WOULD HE SET A FIRE, THEN STAY THERE TO BURN UP?

Allie shook her head. She couldn't answer that question any more than the others swarming about in her mind. She was trying to sort out the rush of feelings sweeping through her at that moment. She was surprised, bewildered, curious, yes. Excited, even. But mostly, she felt ashamed.

She buried her face in her hands and groaned. She felt like such a fool for trusting Walker, for believing that he was another poor, innocent victim, when he was actually an arsonist and con man, and who knew what else? Childish, vain, silly, blind, pig-headed, brain-dead idiot, she berated herself. She couldn't think of words crummy enough to describe how stupid she had been.

She felt a poke in her side, but she didn't want to look up and face Dub. She was too embarrassed. Another poke dug into her, harder. Finally, she lifted her head from her hands. Dub looked concerned. His lips formed the words "You okay?"

Allie sighed and began to type: NO. She wasn't looking for sympathy, though. She didn't deserve it. I THOUGHT I WAS SO SMART, DUB, AND I AM SO INCREDIBLY STUPID.

Dub was looking at her in confusion, so she typed some more: YOU SENSED SOMETHING WEIRD ABOUT JOHN WALKER FROM THE START. YOU EVEN TRIED TO WARN ME. BUT DID I LISTEN? NO. BECAUSE HE SAID YOU WERE JUST BEING JEALOUS AND I BELIEVED HIM. BECAUSE I WAS SO BUSY THINKING I WAS SPECIAL.

Dub looked uncomfortable. AL, TAKE IT EASY. SO YOU MADE A MISTAKE. SO YOU FORGOT THAT I AM DUB THE WISE AND ALL-KNOWING AND YOU ARE A MERE MORTAL. I'M USED TO IT.

Allie could feel a small smile tugging at the corners of her mouth.

Dub continued typing. YOU CAN BEAT UP ON YOUR-
SELF LATER IF YOU REALLY WANT TO. BUT RIGHT NOW
WE ARE IN MAJOR NEED OF A PLAN.

Allie sniffled back the tears she had been about to
shed. Dub was right. And, boy, was it good to have
him use the word "we."

I THINK WE SHOULD START, he was writing, WITH
THE THINGS WE DO KNOW. THEN PROCEED TO THE
THINGS WE DON'T KNOW.

OKAY, Allie agreed. FIRST OF ALL, JOHN WALKER IS A
GHOST FOR A REASON. HE'S TRYING TO USE ME TO HELP
HIM GET WHATEVER IT IS HE WANTS. IF IT'S NOT TO
FIND HIS KILLER, THEN WHAT IS IT? WHY DID HE SET
ME ON THE TRAIL OF MRS. HOBBS? WHY WAS HE IN HER
HOUSE WHEN IT BURNED DOWN? IF HE SET THE FIRE,
THEN SHE DIDN'T KILL HIM, HE KILLED HIMSELF. WHICH
IS PRETTY DUMB.

Dub scratched his chin in thought. Allie had a sud-
den idea and added: MAYBE MRS. HOBBS *DID* SET THE
FIRE, FIGURING WALKER WOULD GET THE BLAME BE-
CAUSE HE'D DONE IT BEFORE . . .

She stopped, feeling more confused than ever. I
JUST KEEP GOING IN CIRCLES.

WE KNOW WALKER SET THE FIRE THAT BURNED DOWN
HIS BUSINESS, wrote Dub. MAYBE HE SET THE FIRE AT
HOBBS'S HOUSE, TOO. BUT THE SUBJECT OF FIRE KEEPS
COMING UP.

REALLY? GEE, I NEVER NOTICED, Allie answered with a smile.

WE'VE BEEN ASSUMING THAT MRS. HOBBS IS THE FIREBUG, wrote Dub. His eyes were getting wide, and Allie almost expected to see smoke rising from the top of his head, coming from the heat of his brain at work. BUT SUPPOSE IT'S WALKER. HE MELTS THE MICRO-FILM AT THE PERFECT MOMENT SO YOU SUSPECT HOBBS, AND SO YOU CAN'T KEEP GOING AND FIND ANY INCRIM-INATING STUFF ABOUT HIM.

With a mixture of sadness and sudden insight, Allie wrote: I THOUGHT CHIEF RASMUSSEN'S ACCIDENT WAS MRS. HOBBS'S FAULT, BUT MAYBE WALKER DID IT. TO MAKE SURE THE CHIEF COULDN'T TELL ME ANY OF THIS STUFF YOU FOUND OUT.

Dub grimaced. RIGHT. AND IF HE STARTED THOSE OTHER FIRES, HE COULD HAVE STARTED THE ONE AT SCHOOL, TOO.

Allie hadn't thought of that. CAN GHOSTS START FIRES? I GUESS THEY CAN. IT'S LIKE FIRES ARE WALKER'S SPECIALTY.

Dub answered with a sardonic expression: WHETHER HE'S DEAD OR ALIVE.

Allie typed: WALKER SEEMS TO HAVE POWERS WAY BEYOND LUCY'S.

The thought terrified her, in light of her new suspicions about Walker. The idea that Michael might get sucked into Walker's web magnified her fear. She realized then that Dub didn't know about Walker's appearing to Michael and luring him to Mrs. Hobbs's house. Quickly she typed out the whole story.

Dub's expression grew grave. WE'VE GOT TO DO SOMETHING.

Allie responded: WE'VE GOT TO "PUT HIM TO REST." LOOK AT THIS—

She clicked back to the ghost Web site. Dub read intently, then typed: THIS ISN'T VERY SPECIFIC.

Allie made a frustrated face, and he continued: SAY HE'S ONE OF THESE VENGEFUL SPIRITS. HE DOESN'T WANT TO BE PUT TO REST. HE'S HAVING FUN. "ENDUR- ING" HIM IS NO GOOD, ESPECIALLY IF HE'S MESSING WITH MICHAEL. HE'S GOT TO BE "LAID TO REST BY THE LIVING." I GUESS THAT MEANS US.

Allie thought about that, then typed: YEAH, BUT HOW?

Dub grimaced. BEATS ME.

THERE'S ONE PERSON WHO MIGHT BE ABLE TO HELP, wrote Allie.

There was a gleam of excitement in Dub's eye as he typed: ARE YOU THINKING WHAT I THINK YOU'RE THINKING?

YEAH. ONLY MY PARENTS WILL NEVER LET ME GO.

YOU STILL HAVE TO FEED HOOVER TODAY, RIGHT?

Allie thumped Dub on the back in triumph. GOOD THINKING! She thought for a moment and added, BUT YOU MIGHT HAVE TO FEED HER—SHE'S BEEN FREAKING OUT AROUND ME. ANYWAY, LET'S GO. ON THE WAY, WE'LL TAKE A LITTLE DETOUR TO ARMSTRONG STREET.

twenty-two

The computer had allowed them to talk in secret, or so they hoped. But Allie and Dub saw no way around the problem that, from that point forward, probably everything they did and said would be seen and heard by John Walker's ghost. They told Allie's mother that they were going to Mr. Henry's house so Dub could feed Hoover.

"Which is true," Allie said to Dub, unconvincingly, she knew. She felt guilty about lying—or telling half the truth—but didn't know what else to do.

Dub had ridden his bike to her house, so they pedaled together to Armstrong Street. They hid their bikes in the bushes on the border of Mrs. Hobbs's property, and Dub got his first good look at the house.

"Weird," he said. "It's like she never fixed it after the fire."

"I know. Cafeteria ladies probably don't make a whole lot of money, but still . . . It's definitely strange." Allie pointed to the boarded-over, tarp-covered side of the house. "Mike was under there. Walker told him it was a fort."

Dub shook his head. "I still can't figure out why he did that."

"Me neither." Allie looked reluctantly toward the front door. She dreaded facing Mrs. Hobbs again, and she had no idea what was going to happen. She and Dub had talked about having a plan, but now that they were actually at Mrs. Hobbs's house, she realized that was as far as it went. And while she now knew that John Walker was not to be trusted entirely, she still didn't know what role Mrs. Hobbs had played in the whole mess.

"Come on," she said, before she lost what little courage she had mustered up.

For the second time that day, she walked across the lawn and up the porch steps. At least this time Dub was by her side. Together, they peered in the window.

Mrs. Hobbs was sitting in the same place in the living room, staring listlessly at nothing. Her expression was slack, her eyes hollow.

Allie went over to the door and knocked. There was no answer. Dub, who was still watching through the window, mouthed the words "She's just sitting there."

Allie knocked again. Again there was no answer. Motioning to Dub to come with her, she opened the door, and they went inside. Mrs. Hobbs barely reacted. Her eyes flickered briefly toward them, then resumed their study of the air, or the wall, or whatever it was she saw inside her head. She hardly seemed threatening, but Allie had no intention of letting her guard slip.

"Mrs. Hobbs?" she ventured.

Without looking in their direction, Mrs. Hobbs spoke. Her voice was a low croak, with no hint of animation or emotion. "So he's in on it now, too?"

"Do you mean Dub?" Allie asked, surprised. She glanced at Dub, who looked terrified.

Mrs. Hobbs didn't answer, appearing to lose interest.

Allie needed to get Mrs. Hobbs's attention. She decided to ask the question that was foremost in her mind. "Mrs. Hobbs, do you believe in ghosts?"

It was an outlandish question, one that under most circumstances would be met with laughter or scorn. But Mrs. Hobbs answered as if it were the most natural thing in the world. "Of course." After a long pause she added wearily, "And you know why."

Allie's heart began jumping around in her chest. Carefully she said, "I've—met—John Walker."

Mrs. Hobbs seemed unsurprised.

"Do you know why he—John Walker, I mean—would appear to my little brother, Michael, and bring him to your house, and leave him alone under there?" Allie gestured toward the unfinished side of the house. "That's where I found him this morning. Mike's only four," she added. "And he was scared."

For the first time, Mrs. Hobbs's face showed a glimmer of feeling. "Four?" she murmured. "Poor child."

Allie looked at Dub, who was clearly as flabbergasted as she was. Was Mrs. Hobbs, the *Snapping Turtle*, showing what sounded like sympathy for a child?

"I don't know what John Walker wants from me, Mrs. Hobbs," Allie went on. "But I really don't like him scaring Mike. What does he want with Mike?"

Mrs. Hobbs seemed to have to gather her strength to respond, and when she did, the answer came slowly and painfully. "I imagine it's another way of trying to hurt me."

Confused, Allie asked, "How?"

Mrs. Hobbs waved this away with a flutter of her hand. "Don't you see? All I have left is my job. He can't stand that I've been promoted. He doesn't want me to have even that tiny little bit of happiness. Ms. Gillespie phoned yesterday to say that your father called her to complain about me. If you hadn't found your brother and he was discovered, or harmed, at my house, I don't think I'd have my job at the school much longer, do you?"

Allie was stunned. She didn't know what she had expected Mrs. Hobbs to say, but certainly not that. "Why doesn't he want you to be happy?" she whispered. "And what does he want with *me*?"

"Why don't you ask him," Mrs. Hobbs said, sounding exhausted. "He's right behind you."

"Yikes!" Dub shouted. Allie, also startled, whirled around.

"I don't see anything," Dub said. He sounded really spooked, and his eyes were just about bugging out of his head.

Allie said quietly, "I do."

She'd known for several weeks that ghosts truly did exist. But she'd never before seen one, not a whole one, anyway, if "whole" was a word that could be used to describe a ghost. For the first time she was looking at John Walker, and not just his face but his entire body—his entire ghost body. He wasn't solid, like a real person, because sometimes Allie could see right through him to the wall behind.

He turned his dark eyes on her and pleaded, "*Listen to me, Allie. Don't believe her! She's the one who ruined my life. All I ever wanted was a home and a family, and look at me. She did this to me.*"

"She set the fire?" Allie asked. "The one that killed you and her husband and her baby? The reason I ask is because I know you burned down your business for the insurance money."

There was a silence, during which John Walker's face went through a series of contortions. Outrage, wounded innocence, and frustration passed over his features, ending with what appeared to Allie to be an angry pout.

Mrs. Hobbs asked quietly, "What's your answer, John?"

While Allie waited for Walker to answer, she sneaked a look at Dub. When she saw his face, she realized that he couldn't see *or hear* John Walker, and he was dying to know what was going on. But there was no time to fill him in.

Walker burst out furiously, *"It was your fault, and you know it!"*

"That's true in a way, John," said Mrs. Hobbs thoughtfully. "It's my own fault I got mixed up with you in the first place. I was young and foolish. And I've had the rest of my life to regret it."

"No," Walker said angrily. *"We were happy. Then you ruined everything. I'll never be able to forget what you did to me!"* Walker's voice was high now, and trembling with emotion.

"I did nothing except come to my senses before I

married you. How could you think I'd want you after you bragged about burning down your own business for the money?"

"I did it for us! You said you loved me—and then you jilted me! You married him. You had a baby, and a happy life, and I had nothing!"

Compared to Walker's near-hysteria, Mrs. Hobbs sounded calm, almost detached. "Poor John. You're always the victim, aren't you?"

"You deserted me! I needed you! You had no right!" Turning to Allie, he said, *"She made me do it. You see that, don't you?"*

"You set fire to her house and killed her husband and baby because she broke up with you?" Allie asked incredulously.

Hearing that, Dub, apparently unable to contain himself any longer, shouted, "But *he* died in that fire, too! It doesn't make sense!"

"It does if you know John Walker," said Mrs. Hobbs. "He's careless. Thoughtless enough and careless enough to die in the fire he set with his own hand. I only wish I'd died then, too."

"Don't say that!" Allie protested.

"It's true. Ever since I broke our engagement and married Clifford, he's done everything he could to make my life miserable. Then he got you to help him do his dirty work. Now you say he's using your little brother, too. It's got to stop." Turning to Walker, she said, "No more children are going to be hurt. You win, John. I give up."

"*No!*" Allie cried. "He can't win. We can't let him."

"I hope you'll be able to appreciate the irony, John," Mrs. Hobbs went on, as if Allie hadn't spoken. "When I die—"

"You're not going to die!" Allie insisted.

"Nobody's dying!" Dub shouted, sounding—and looking—scared.

"When I die," Mrs. Hobbs continued, "it's over for you, too. Without me to torment, you've got no reason to exist. Without me, you have no target for your pathetic jealousy and revenge. I don't mind dying, John, to put an end to you."

Allie couldn't bear to listen. She turned to Walker and shouted angrily, "Why don't you just go away and leave her alone! Leave us all alone!"

"*No, Allie,*" he said soothingly. "*I can't do that. She's got to pay for what she did.*"

"For what *I* did, John?" Mrs. Hobbs shook her head sadly.

"*It was your fault,*" Walker repeated. "*You made me do it.*" To Allie he said cajolingly, "*You believe me, don't you? It's the truth.*"

"The truth!" Mrs. Hobbs said scornfully. "What would you know about the truth?"

Walker glared at Mrs. Hobbs, and Allie thought she had never seen such malice.

"You couldn't bear to hear the truth," Mrs. Hobbs said bitterly. "And I've lived alone with it for far too long."

Allie couldn't stand any longer to hear Mrs. Hobbs talk about dying. It wasn't right—it was all backward! Walker had to give up, not Mrs. Hobbs. Allie moved between Mrs. Hobbs and John Walker's ghost. She needed to engage Mrs. Hobbs's full attention. "Mrs. Hobbs," she said loudly and, she hoped, firmly. "You're not going to die to stop him. There's got to be some other way."

"There's *got* to be," Dub repeated urgently.

Mrs. Hobbs looked at Allie, really looked at her, for the first time that day. Slowly, she gazed at Dub, then back at Allie. "You seem to mean well, children, but there's more to this story"—she stopped and sighed deeply—"than you can possibly know." She added sadly, "More than you two youngsters should have to know."

Allie didn't have any idea what Mrs. Hobbs was talking about. But she couldn't let Mrs. Hobbs die to put an end to Walker's ghost. There had to be another way to lay him to rest. There *had* to be.

Looking at Mrs. Hobbs sitting forlornly in the shabby living room, Allie had a sudden, clear glimpse into what Mrs. Hobbs's life was like outside school. Allie had told the class that was what she wanted to find out, and now she knew. Mrs. Hobbs lived a sad and solitary life, tortured by the memories of her husband and child and the vindictive ghost of John Walker. It was almost more than Allie could bear.

She whispered, "Mrs. Hobbs, we"—she pointed to Dub, including him as she continued to speak slowly—"we didn't know you before, but now we do. A little, anyway. So it's not like you have to be—alone—anymore."

Mrs. Hobbs listened, and an odd expression came over her face. Allie sneaked a glance at Walker, and wished she hadn't. He was looking right at her, and the fury on his face almost took her breath, and her courage, away. She could actually feel the heat of his anger.

Trying to ignore him, Allie said desperately, "We'll help you get rid of him. What can we do?"

His voice shaking with anger and disbelief, Walker said, *"Not you, too! I counted on you. You said I could trust you. Don't you betray me, too."*

Allie put her hands over her ears to block out Walker's ranting. The room was growing hot, and Allie felt a stab of real fear at the power of his rage.

"Tell her, Evelyn," Walker was saying. *"Tell her how sorry she'll be if she betrays me."*

"Don't listen to him," Allie cried, grasping Mrs. Hobbs's shoulder to keep her attention. "Think! How can we stop him?"

At Allie's touch, Mrs. Hobbs appeared to rouse

herself from her stupor. Her eyes lost their dullness as they focused on Allie's face. She nodded, seeming to make a decision. When she spoke, her voice was no longer sluggish and detached but steady and firm. "You know, John," she said, "there's a part to our story you've never known. I never told you, partly because I was afraid of what you'd do with the knowledge. I was afraid if the truth got out, I'd lose my job at the school."

"What are you talking about?" Walker said impatiently.

"And, strange as it sounds, part of me didn't want to tell you because, well, I thought I loved you once. And even though you won't believe it, I never wanted to hurt you."

Walker snorted with disgust, but Mrs. Hobbs's eyes never wavered as she continued talking. "Clifford Hobbs taught me what real love is."

Walker's face darkened with fury. *"I can't understand how you could have preferred that pathetic old fossil to me."*

"Of course you can't. Because all you know is your own petty jealousy. You don't know what it means to be decent and kind and forgiving. Clifford did."

"Don't talk to me about Clifford!" Walker screamed.

"But I have to, John, if you're going to know the

truth. You see, when you and I were engaged, I discovered that I was going to have a baby. But then I found out what kind of man you were and knew I could never marry you. I was prepared to take the consequences and raise my baby alone. Then I met Clifford, and he asked me to marry him. I told him I was going to have a baby, and he said he'd be proud to marry me and give that baby a home and a name. And he did." Mrs. Hobbs was weeping as she said, "Clifford loved Tommy as if he were his own son."

There was a terrible silence then. Allie was trying hard to understand everything Mrs. Hobbs had been saying, but she was distracted by the look of horror that had slowly taken over John Walker's face.

Mrs. Hobbs put her face in her hands. "Tommy was *your* son, John. And you—you—" She stopped, and began to sob.

Allie stiffened with shock as her mind filled in the words Mrs. Hobbs had been unable to say.

The room had been growing hotter and hotter, and a bellow of anguish unlike anything Allie had ever heard resounded from the walls: "*Noooo!*" It rang in Allie's ears and pierced her heart.

At the same time, she was aware of Dub shouting frantically, "Allie, what the heck is going on?"

She wanted to answer, but was unable to speak as, before her disbelieving eyes, the paint on the wall behind Mrs. Hobbs's couch began to bubble and blister and peel. Then the squares of linoleum beneath Allie's feet began to curl. The lampshade on the table seemed to be melting, and next to it, the leaves of a potted plant withered and turned brown. Sweat ran down Allie's face and into her eyes as she watched a plastic cup ooze into a puddle on the windowsill. The heat was so intense that each breath she took seared her throat and lungs.

Gasping for air, she turned to the ghost of John Walker and saw to her amazement that he had begun slowly to disintegrate.

His hands and feet became blurry and indistinct, then disappeared altogether. His body contorted, and he continued to moan, *"No, no, no, no . . ."* His face hung suspended in midair, his expression one of unspeakable agony. Finally, only his dark, tortured eyes remained, burning into Allie's for what seemed a long, long time, before flickering, at last, into oblivion.

Allie, Mrs. Hobbs, and Dub remained frozen in stunned silence as the room slowly cooled around them.

twenty-three

Dub was the first one to speak. In a shaking voice he whispered, "What happened? Is he gone?"

Allie looked into his ashen face and nodded. They both turned to the quiet form of Mrs. Hobbs, who was staring with disbelief at the place where John Walker's ghost had been. "Gone?" she repeated. Then again, wonderingly, "He's gone . . ."

Allie tried to shake herself free of the spell that Mrs. Hobbs's terrible story had cast over her. She felt almost overwhelmed by sorrow and pity and horror. At that moment she wanted more than anything to run from that strange, sad house and never come back. But how could she just walk away? She felt she should speak to Mrs. Hobbs about what had happened, yet she had no idea what to say. If there were words suitable for the situation in which they found themselves, Allie didn't know what they were.

The silence stretched on. Finally, Mrs. Hobbs turned to look first at Allie, then at Dub, then back at Allie. "Who would ever believe what just happened?" she murmured hoarsely. "I can hardly take it in myself."

Allie merely nodded. She knew very well the feeling of being part of something that the rest of the world could barely imagine, let alone accept as true. She thought about what Mrs. Hobbs had said. "No one would believe it," she answered slowly. "And what good would it do to tell anyone, anyway?"

Dub and Mrs. Hobbs both looked at her, waiting for her to go on.

"Maybe," she said, thinking as she spoke, "we should keep John Walker's secret. We could . . . lay it to rest . . . along with his ghost."

A glimmer of surprise, and hope, passed over Mrs. Hobbs's face. Almost fearfully, she asked, "Could we really do that?"

Allie looked at Dub, who said solemnly, "I think it would be the best thing for everybody."

Mrs. Hobbs seemed to think it over, then nodded in agreement. "Thank you," she said simply.

There didn't seem to be anything else to say. Allie met Dub's eyes. It was time to go. They began walking toward the door. Allie turned back to say softly, "We'll see you at school tomorrow."

It hung like a question in the air, and for a moment Allie was afraid there would be no answer.

"Yes," said Mrs. Hobbs at last, and Allie heard a hint of something like happiness in her voice. "I'll see you at school." A flash of apprehension crossed her face. "Unless Ms. Gillespie . . ." Her words trailed off, and Allie immediately knew what she was thinking.

"Don't worry," Allie said quickly. "I'll explain that it was all a misunderstanding." She thought for a moment, then added, "Oh, and, Mrs. Hobbs? I've decided to interview my grandmother for Elders Day." She paused. "So *your* secrets will be safe, too."

Allie and Dub walked across Mrs. Hobbs's lawn to their bikes. There was so much to say that Allie didn't know where to begin, so she just asked, "To Mr. Henry's house?" Dub nodded, and they rode along in silence, both deep in thought about what they had just witnessed.

When they pulled into Mr. Henry's driveway and around to the back door, Allie said, "This will be the true test."

"You mean Hoover will be able to tell if Walker's really dead? Or whatever you call it when a ghost croaks?"

"Yeah."

"From what I saw and heard, I don't think you've got anything to worry about," Dub replied.

He started toward the door, but Allie held on to his arm to stop him. "Dub," she said, "thanks for going over there with me."

"No problem," Dub answered. "I'm glad I went. For the few seconds when I wasn't scared out of my wits, it was pretty interesting."

"Talk about scared! Just be glad you couldn't see Walker! Although I bet it was awful not being able to see or hear, and just having to *imagine* what was going on."

"You got that right," said Dub.

"Anyway, Dub, I feel really stupid about that fight we had. Or whatever it was."

"Forget it."

"All right, but there's one thing I want to say first, okay? If you want to be friends with Pam, it's all right. She's nice. I was just, well, jealous, I guess."

"Well, as long as we're having true confessions, how about me?" Dub said. "I was jealous of a *ghost*."

They both giggled. "But it isn't funny, really," Allie said with a shudder, "when you think about it. Walker did those horrible things all because he couldn't stand it that Mrs. Hobbs married somebody else."

"It's sickening," said Dub. "If you ever catch me acting jealous again, just call me John. I promise I'll snap right out of it."

Allie held out her hand for a high-five. "It's a deal."

"Well," said Dub, pointing to the door. "Shall we go in and see if you earn the Hoover Seal of Approval?"

"Okay," said Allie, more confidently than she felt. It wasn't easy to forget the sight of Hoover growling at her, teeth bared, hackles raised in fear.

She reached under the flowerpot for the key, but before putting it in the lock she said, "Dub? I wonder . . . how come we both acted so weird."

Dub, who ordinarily had an answer for everything, was silent. If Allie wasn't mistaken, she saw a faint blush color his neck. That gave her the courage to say, "I think I got so jealous because I thought you liked Pam better. Liked her, you know, for a girlfriend."

"Are you serious?" asked Dub, looking surprised. "She's nice, but no way."

Allie went on, feeling—she couldn't believe it—*shy* in front of Dub. "But why did it bug me so much? It's not like *I'm* your girlfriend." She paused and added, "Right?"

As soon as she had spoken, she wished she could snatch the words back. What if Dub looked at her as if she were crazy and said again, "No way!" She'd feel like a complete idiot.

Dub's blush crept from his neck to his face. "Who said you're not?"

Allie laughed happily. "Nobody," she said.

They stood grinning at each other for a moment. Then Allie turned to the door and opened it. Glancing back at Dub, she said, "Ready?"

"Go for it."

Allie stepped into the kitchen, followed by Dub. "Hoover?" she called. She crossed her fingers and looked at Dub hopefully as they listened to the thump of Hoover's footsteps on the floor overhead, then the click of her toenails as she descended the stairs. She burst into the kitchen with her head high, her tail wagging, and her mouth open in a doggy grin.

"Hoover!" Allie exclaimed joyfully. "Come here, girl!"

She fell to her knees so she could rub Hoover's soft ears and bury her face in the big dog's warm, sweet-smelling fur. "You were way smarter than I was, Hoovey," she said. "Next time I suspect there's a ghost around, I'm coming straight to you to check it out!"

"I don't see how you can even *think* about another ghost," said Dub. "If I were you, I'd be sending out vibes saying, 'This ghost magnet is out of business.' "

"Believe me," said Allie, stroking Hoover's big,

shaggy head, "I'm in no hurry to meet another John Walker. All I'm saying is, if there *is* a next time, I'm not going to be so . . ." She paused, searching for the right word. "Gullible," she said finally.

Dub looked at her, a serious expression on his face. "Did you know *gullible* is the only word that isn't in the dictionary?"

"Really?" Allie asked. Then she caught herself. "You rat," she said, giving Dub a playful swat.

Dub was cracking up. "Almost got you," he said gleefully.

"Almost," Allie said. "See? I'm learning." She got up and began pouring dog food into Hoover's dish.

"What about Mike?" Dub asked. "What if he sees another ghost?"

"I'm going to tell him that if he ever sees somebody who looks 'funny' the way the 'nice' man did, he should tell me about it. That way, the next ghost—"

"If there is a next ghost," Dub added.

"—will have not only Mike, but you, and me, and Hoover, and Mrs. Hobbs to contend with," Allie finished, feeling pleased with the idea. "And by now, the spook world ought to know better than to mess with us!"

Dub and Allie watched Hoover as she crunched away at her dinner. "Hey!" said Dub suddenly.

"You're really going to interview your grandmother, then?"

"Yeah, I guess. Karen will say I chickened out, but so what?" Allie shrugged. "After everything that's happened, it's hard to imagine letting Karen Laver bother me ever again."

"I know what you mean," Dub agreed. Then he offered a wicked grin. "And about Elders Day, don't forget"—he raised his voice and finished at the top of his lungs—"*you can always interview Louie Howell.*"

"For Pete's sake, Dub, you'll wake the dead!" exclaimed Allie. She smiled and added, "We wouldn't want to do that now, would we?"